# Stars
### and
# Ghosts

## Daniel DiQuinzio

**BLUE FORGE PRESS**
Port Orchard ✲ Washington

Stars and Ghosts
Copyright 2024
by Daniel DiQuinzio

First eBook Edition June 2025
First Print Edition June 2025

ISBN 979-8-89439-048-2



For information about film, reprint or other subsidiary rights, contact: blueforgegroup@gmail.com



Blue Forge Press is the print division of the volunteer-run, federal 501(c)3 nonprofit, Blue Legacy (EIN 83-4307421), founded in 1989 and dedicated to supporting artisans marginalized due to race, age, disability, economics or other factors. We strive to empower storytellers from all walks of life with our four divisions: Blue Forge Press, Blue Forge Films, Blue Forge Gaming, and Blue Forge Sound. Find out more at www.BlueForgeGroup.org

Blue Forge Press
7419 Ebbert Drive Southeast
Port Orchard, Washington 98367
blueforgepress@gmail.com
360-550-2071 ph.txt

# Table of Contents

# Stars

### and

# Ghosts

## Daniel DiQuinzio

# Lady in the Black Dress

anessa Chang's terrified eyes starred behind her at the terrifying and amorphous form, which seemed to be half on the road and half on the sidewalk, as it hovered menacingly towards her over the asphalt towards her while she raced down Boylston Street in Boston to escape from it. She feared she would not live to marry her fiancé if this monster captured her, because she dreaded it desired to consume not only her body but also her vey soul. Vanessa swung her head around. In response, the Catholic cross that she always wore, even at the club where she worked as a dancer, as a sign of her devotion to her Catholic faith to swing backwards whacking itself against the tops of her breasts. Her plan of escape required her to reach the Green Line station at Boylston, at which she could find safety inside from her other worldly stalker. As she moved, she felt the sole of her left foot rub against the small lift she always wore inside of her left high heel, which compensated for Vanessa being born with her left leg several inches shorter than her right leg. On this night, she was unconcerned with having been born both physically and intellectually disabled—she was also born with dyslexia—for she knew the only things that mattered right now were the survival of herself and her immortal soul.

Her feet hit the pavement in her black platform high heels. She groaned. Vanessa's body hurt because her flight through the torrential rain was going on for many minutes now. In addition, she was beginning to feel a physical discomfort as the hem of her long dark black evening dress rubbed against her legs. Between her moans of pain, Vanessa cursed her choice of attire. Then she remembered she could not have known at the conclusion of her shift at the club that she would need to run for her life. Tonight, was her anniversary. Two years ago tonight, she wore this same dress and the high heels on the very first date with the man whose name she would soon take as her own, which involved them spending the evening at the local arcade. They planned to celebrate their anniversary when Vanessa arrived home. Now the completion of those plans and their becoming man and wife all depended upon one thing, which was Vanessa staying alive and successfully reaching the station that was her destination.

Despite everything, she felt Vanessa forced herself to press forward. "Help me, please!" she screamed. "Please, help me. It is a he or a she, and it is after me. Somebody please…. anybody please help me."

There was no response. She was greatly disappointed but she was also not surprised that no brave man or woman came running to rescue her. According to her wristwatch, it was now almost ten at night, and on this night, an intense summer storm was hitting the city. As a result, there would be no one out near Downtown Boston or Boston Commons, which was the largest and oldest public park in the city, to come to her aid.

The falling rain battered away at Vanessa's dark brown coat, making her once more despair at having lost her umbrella in Boston Commons. Within her mind, there was a brief temptation to stop to rest. She could not. Right now, she greatly feared if she slowed down at all, the beast would finally catch up to her and then it would be the end of everything for her.

Once more, she forced her dark black eyes to peer over her shoulders at the creature, which caused her such great distress. Vanessa took in the form of this horrifying specter, which was comprised of a collection of three circular and immaterial clouds that were made from a mixture of dark black charcoal and bright white soot. Her skin crawled. Scattered through them were dashes of bright red and bright pink ash. Moving around the outer edges of them a collection of several sets of small black, red and white puffs of smoke could be seen along with a combination of trails of black and white smoke, which were all dangling from the clouds.

She shuddered because it was drawing ever closer to her on this rainy night. Vanessa turned around to look ahead and continued moving because she did not want to become a very attractive meal for it with her soul becoming the desert. She would also never see Richard, her finance, again. He was the handsome historian who was waiting with open arms in the apartment they resided in within the North End of Boston for her to return to him. She loved him deeply. Their engagement was one year old now and the date for their wedding was scheduled for the first Sunday in November. Vanessa knew there was only option open to her if she wanted to become Mrs. Richard Casey and that was for her to arrive alive at the station at Boylston for the Green Line, which was the Boston version of trolley cars.

Vanessa moved ahead. With her eyes, she took notice of the street sign hanging in the distance. She tried to study it because it was important for her to know if she was coming to Tremont Street, the cross street that was located just before Boylston Station, which would inform her of whether or not she was moving in the right direction. Vanessa squinted her eyes. Due to the rain, the white lettering on the sign blended into the green background making it hard for her to learn the name of the street. Her lips murmured in annoyance at her dyslexia, which she was diagnosed with as a little girl, caused her mind to swap the order of the letters in the name around and created a new name for a brand new street. Alas, that street was located nowhere in the city making Vanessa abandon her efforts.

While she considered her next move, she suddenly felt a new pain in her shoulder, coming from her purse flying backwards to hit her in the shoulders. Vanessa ignored it. The pain in her feet was steadying increasing as her high heels moved rapidly over the wet pavement. Her heart pounded forcing her to accept she was desperate enough to make a second attempt at summoning aid. "Is there anyone out there?!" she cried. "Help me please, help me please anybody help me!" Vanessa screamed. "Is any one out there? Help me, please... Any body, please... Please help me."

As before, there was no reply to her distress call. Vanessa sighed. The rain attacked her coat and opened a second front in its war against her by giving an intense pelting to the long black bun into which she tied her long black hair into before departing the club. The physical agony increased. It was also now spreading outwards from her feet to the rest of her small body becoming slowly harder for her to ignore.

Between splashes of water on her high heels, Vanessa wondered if her dyslexia was responsible for the terror she faced or if it was instead merely terrible luck. Inspired by that thought, she recalled the beginning of how she ended up in this situation. Vanessa was born nearly twenty-seven years ago in Boston. She grew up in Chinatown, where her parents owned a business, which was a combination of dry cleaners and tailoring business. She was the second oldest child. In her childhood, Vanessa fell in love with the theater, and hoped to one day have a career in it as an actress but the dyslexia ended those dreams, because her condition made it very hard for her to learn any new skills or to learn any new information from books. It also caused her to drop out of school.

Out of a desire to help their oldest daughter, Mr. and Mrs. Change employed Vanessa at the store doing menial tasks, which did not require much reading. They also paid her to perform the additional duty of serving as a human mannequin whenever Mrs. Chang needed to make alternations to feminine items of clothing. Within a few years, Vanessa was also appearing in advertisements for the family business. However, she was slowly becoming very frustrated about still living at home with her parents.

After she turned twenty-one, a friend informed her several of the local strip clubs and burlesque clubs where holding auditions for new dancers and that the performers received very generous wages and tips. Inspired by that information, Vanessa remembered her long forgotten dreams of being in the theater and chose to audition to be a dancer at one of the burlesque clubs, because she felt she would be a natural performer having practiced various forms of dance since she was a little girl. In addition, she was excited to have finally found a well paying job that did not require any book learning. The audition was easy to pass. A few months into her career as a burlesque dancer, Vanessa accumulated enough money that she could finally move out of the family dwelling and into her own apartment in Beacon Hill.

Mr. and Mrs. Chang were very disturbed by her choice of profession. They expected Vanessa to set the proper example for her younger sisters; she was there oldest daughter, by entering a respectful profession and marrying well. Their vocal protests of their daughter earning an income through dancing and removing her clothes on stage to entertain men muted somewhat after she accepted Richard's proposal of marriage. They were very pleased with her choice of a future husband. Vanessa and Richard first met at the club over two years ago when he came in one night with several of his class mates from Boston University, where he was studying history, to celebrate the end of their semester by having dinner and a round of drinks as they watched the dancers perform. Richard was so smitten with Vanessa's beauty as she danced on stage; his first visit occurred was during her shift, which he requested to speak with her in the privacy of her dressing room. Shortly afterwards they began to date.

Vanessa heard several sounds ending her recollections of her life and brought her back to the current moment. Raindrops continued attacking her while her high heels passed through one puddle after another. She was beginning to feel very tired, which made Vanessa hope she was finally drawing close to the warmth and shelter of Boylston Station. Over the falling rain, the movements of the large hands on street clock on Tremont Street were audible as they ticked away. Now, it was almost ten at night.

Once more Vanessa peered over her shoulder seeing to her extreme distress that her inhuman stalker was almost on top of her. She noticed something new. The circular clouds, at its core, were now all glowing a bright combination of gold and white. Her eyes watched in horror as the colors spread out from them passing through the puffs at the perimeter of the creature's form and through the multiple smoky vapors dangling off the monstrous being.

Vanessa could learn nothing more. She brought her head around making her Catholic cross, bounce on the chain around her neck before swinging backwards into her chest. Without a doubt, she now knew the only way to ensure she returned to the man she loved was to outpace her would be attacker. That seemed to be an impossible task to accomplish. Vanessa's lungs panted heavily as she forced her feet and her legs to move over the wet concrete for it was certain if they froze up she would soon be chewed apart by this demonic apparition as its long awaited late night feast. As she ran, something hit her in the face. Vanessa grunted. She was dismayed to learn her black hair bun was losing its cohesion under the constant bombardment from the rain and was now breaking apart into the individual strands, which fell down over her eyes blocking her vision. Her fingers brushed the strands aside.

Fate soon rewarded Vanessa for her persistence with the appearance of another green street sign, which lay ahead of on her course down Boylston Street. She tried to read it. Following several minutes of valiant effort, she accepted it was impossible for her to deduce the street name courtesy of her dyslexia. Instead, she turned to an old coping habit. That was navigating using set of familiar landmarks and as such, she scanned the area with her eyes, seeking any recognizable building or identifiable business that could tell if she was getting close to Boylston Station. The one she found was a brown square brick building with a sign hanging above its entrance that was comprised of a green line above a white line.

Vanessa's eyes lit up knowing she was fast approaching a Green Line Station but at this distance even if she was not born with dyslexia, she could not deduce the name. That did not matter. As long as she could get on the D Line or the E Line, she could take the subway line to the station at Haymarket, which was as the large transit station in the North End, and from there it was only a few minutes walk to the apartment. Vanessa smiled delighted to know she was only a minute away from her salvation.

For a second time, Vanessa's thoughts raced as she resumed recounting how she found herself in this trying situation. Normally after her shift ended, she took the Orange Line, one of the Boston subways, to the station at Haymarket. Over the last month, the Orange Line service in Downtown Boston was suspended due to maintenance being performed on the tracks, which forced her to travel to the nearest Green Line station at Park Street and the only way to reach Park Street from the club was to pass through Boston Commons. Tonight, due to the rain, Vanessa soon found her course was instead leading her through the Southwest portion of the park where the Greet Elm Tree once stood several centuries ago. There, she felt a strange presence behind her. At the time, she expected it to be a man who was following her with the intention of mugging her, attacking her or performing some other very hideous act upon her.

Vanessa spun around to defend herself and it was then she discovered the horrendous sight. In fright, Vanessa stumbled backwards in her high heels and dropped her umbrella beside her. Shortly afterwards the primal instincts for survival, which were passed down to her through the previous generations of the women in her family line, took over body making her move as if she were a lighting bolt over the wet grass to escape from this great danger. To her dismay in her haste, she made the mistake of running in the wrong direction bringing her further away from Park Street instead of towards it. The being gave chase. As a result, Vanessa soon realized reversing her course was not an option forcing her to continue to the station at Boylston.

Clicks of her high heels and the splashing of water on them brought, Vanessa out of her memories. She came to the station. Her heart warmed knowing in only a few seconds she would be safe and would soon be on her way home to her beloved Richard. As she approached the entrance, Vanessa stepped into a large puddle and both of her high heels slipped on the water making her stumble and lose her balance. She fell forward. Acting solely upon instinct, she stuck her hands out in front of her to cushion her fall thereby preventing her head from hitting the pavement when she landed face first in the puddle.

She lay there. It took Vanessa several seconds to recover from both the feelings of embarrassment about her collapse and the anger at herself that her own careless caused her defeat on the edge of reaching her sanctuary. She spun onto her back. While the water dripped on her, Vanessa sensed something was different in the area around her but it was unrelated to her being sopping wet. She raised her head looking out through her long wet black hair, and she was horrified to find her inhuman stalker ceased its movement and was holding station just beyond the spot where she sat.

As she struggled to breathe, Vanessa found her eyes were strangely drawn to the see through outline of this demonic collection of smoke. She trembled. The fact that it was merely hovering over the sidewalk did nothing to make her feel any less terrified that it would soon end her. Vanessa's instincts for survival took control of her body. She hurriedly reached over to her purse, which fell off her shoulder during her dramatic collapse, because she was seeking to retrieve the loaded ladies handgun she always carried inside of it to aid in the protection of her person. She gripped the zipper. Vanessa's fingers slipped as she struggled to open her purse forcing her to abandon that particular plan to protect her from this demon.

Following that failure, her up bringing in the Catholic Church took control of her mind resulting in her left hand coming up to her face where her fingers horizontally and then vertically over her dark black eye as she made the sign of the cross. It was her hope to convince the Almighty father to intervene on this stormy night and rescue her from becoming a very petite and lovely feast for this evil form. Vanessa recited the Lord's Prayer. Even if she could not avoid a very disturbing fate on Earth, she was praying the Almighty could be persuaded to act to protect her everlasting soul, which would ensure she could one day be reunited in Heaven with her beloved Richard. Her hand came down to her chest. There she repeated the action of making the sign of the cross by running her fingers over her heart seeking to increase the chances of her creator hearing her prayers and acting to protect her from a very deadly encounter with this monstrous being. Once again, she recited the Lord's Prayer.

The monstrous blob retreated. Vanessa was confused as this never happened before during her mad flight away from it to protect her vey existence. While water trickled off her body, she wondered if maybe her prayers were answered and the Almighty was now acting to protect his mortal child by fighting this evil. Vanessa lay there. Her eyes were locked in horror on it forcing her to fully see as it ominously shone brightly through the rain on the dark night, which she feared indicated it was preparing to eat its prey, following the conclusion of its hunt.

That would not occur. Vanessa decided to take advantage of the brief lull in the situation and quickly put some more distance between her and monster. She tried to stand up but her high heels slipped again on the water spending her spiraling back down into the puddle. Vanessa cursed. After pushing her high heels into the ground, she reached behind her with her arms to drag and push her body backwards through the puddle to the other side. There she stopped and starred outwards seeing the immaterial being began to under go a startling metamorphoses.

The outer two of the circles comprising the main part of the creature's body split in half but all of the white, red and black puffs around it remained stationary and so did all of the smoky vapors. Vanessa's skin crawled. She felt as if a deep state of fear was starting to spread through her body forcing her to breathe to prevent herself from freezing within the puddle. The central circle contracted. Her blood raced as she witnessed the outer circles continue to change by expanding lengthwise and at the same time contracting as they assumed a more slimmer and slender appearance. Of course, that was before they stunned her by disconnecting from each other and then reconnecting in a manner, which stacked them on top of each other.

Vanessa watched the demon grow two lengthy arms followed by what appeared to be a pair of very long and slender legs and it made her feel as if her blood was turning cold at the sight. Before her eyes, a pair of immaterial hands and feet emerged from the outer circles with out stretched digits functioning as the ghostly version of fingers and toes. Vanessa was shocked but that was before two small mounds emerged and then the lines of black smoke floated over to the top and connected to it creating an image of long black charcoal hair. Afterwards impossible occurred, as a face composed of bright white smoke emerged at the top of the creature.

Before Vanessa's eyes, the transformation continued with the collection of multi colored puffs surrounding this spectral imitation of a being began to dissolve. Several puffs of black smoke moved down to the outlines of its ghastly feet encasing them in an outline of two black high heels. As for the red puffs, they moved to the face and the tips of its translucent fingers and there as Vanessa watched, they merged with the existing structure creating the image of some ghastly form of decoration. She screamed. The unfolding events increased the great terror felt by her at this moment, when the remaining black puffs along with all of the white puffs surrounded this demon's front and its rear creating the image of it now wearing an outline of two items of feminine clothing.

The light within the apparition increased by several volumes glowing brighter than ever before. There was a brief explosion, which forced Vanessa to cover her eyes with her hands to protect herself from it. Seconds later she dropped them. As she starred across the puddle, she was horrified to see the alterations of specter were complete and the being that previously stalked her now appeared to be the smoke and ash equivalent of the body of a young woman.

At first, Vanessa thought it was attempting to emulate her appearance as a prelude to draining her soul from her body but this nameless spirit made no movement and merely hung there. It was as if its essence were suspended in the air by invisible strings while it shone the night illuminating the area around the Green Line station. Her eyes observed the imitation of clothing that covered its essence. The outfit the ghost fashioned to clad herself in was comprised of a long black dress, which hung over a bright white women's blouse. Although it was an archaic and ancient design, Vanessa knew it was very familiar causing a sinking feeling to spread through her that she should recognize it.

Her eyes looked up further letting her study the face of the ghost. Near the top of it were two round smears of bright red paint, which seemed to resemble eyes. They opened starring at her. In the middle, she found a long stretch of bright pink ink looking as if this was a pair of lips. They parted. What was more shocking was that, this specter then multiple times opened and closed her mouth as if she were attempting to moan in extreme pain.

Vanessa forced herself to remain calm. It was then she realized this conjured essence was not advancing towards her allowing her the time to get herself back onto her own two high heels. She retrieved her purse and it occurred to her that now was the opportune moment to finally make good on her escape. She hesitated. The sense of horror that previously existed within her faded away which was replaced by a morbid combination of curiosity and a compelling desire for answers. Together they overwhelmed her instincts and prompted Vanessa to advance forward having decided she would subject this ghost to the questions that she was wondering since her flight began. "Who are you?" she asked.

"My name isn't of interest to you," the lady answered. "It no longer matters."

Vanessa's eyes widen processing what just occurred. She did not think the ghost possessed the capacity to comprehend her questions yet alone that it was possible for it to posses the ability to make any response. "You've got to have a name," she stated. "What're you called?"

"My name is no longer important. I'm not remembered by the name that I was born with for now I'm only remembered for my crimes on this Earth."

"Why've have you come here?"

"My spirit has dwelt here in this area of the city since long before you or any of the current inhabits of this city were born."

"What do you want?"

"I merely sought to make my presence known to you upon this night."

"Why've you been chasing me?"

"I apologized if I scared you, whenever I encounter anyone in this part of the city I'm compelled to seek to establish contact with them."

"But those things, which I saw earlier, those circles what're they?"

"They were a manifestation of my essence."

"They couldn't have been. They were circles, not a human being."

"That was the earliest stage of my efforts to create a representation of the physical form I once possessed in life."

Vanessa studied the form closer discovering there were brown blotches scattered just beneath the face, which placed them where the neck would be located on this strange being if she were still human. She did not notice them earlier. Beyond them being the same shade as several kinds of rope, they did not provide Vanessa with any information about how what was once clearly a woman came to be a ghost or how she came to be in this part of Boston.

Vanessa pondered the ghost's statements. In addition, she also saw through the style of the image of her dress, wondering why she swore she saw it before and where she was when it occurred. Then at last it occurred to her, that of course, it was a lady's pirate outfit. Vanessa felt she should have comprehended that at the first glance as she danced in a more revealing outfit of a such a costume several times before at the club and performed in it several times in the privacy of the bedroom for Richard.

The statements of this undead woman were slowing causing more queries to form with in Vanessa's mind, which she felt must be posed to this phantom. "Why've you come here?" she questioned.

"I haunt this area of the city through every moment of every day and every night as the punishment that I now pay for the crimes and the sins I committed during my life."

"What do you mean?"

"In my life I violated the laws of man and nature through undertaking horrible acts against my brothers and sisters. Now I must pay for them."

Within her mind, the natural reaction to this woman's statements caused Vanessa to remember an old legend Richard told her several times about the dark nickname the early inhabitants of Boston gave to The Great Elm. They called it the hanging tree. Recalling that name, caused a lesson Vanessa learned in elementary school about the very disturbing history of The Great Elm, this tree stood in Boston Commons before it burned down in 1837, to resurface in her mind. For some time, in the early centuries of the cities history it was common for members of the cities judiciary to punish those convicted of high crimes through sentencing them to die and often the ordered form of execution was them hanging from ropes tied to the branches of the tree. Whatever acts this dame once committed, she must have died in that manner.

"I've walked through Boston Commons many times," Vanessa stated, "Yet I've never encounter a ghost there before."

"My lingering consciousness haunts the commons and the area surrounding it since my sentence was passed down by the highest judge of all many long decades ago."

"How come I've never seen you before?"

"I'm there trapped between the realms, it's only in this brief window at night allotted to me by the creator that I can make my presence known to those who pass me."

"Who's punishing you?"

"The most powerful being of all."

"What crimes did you commit?"

"In my life through my own choice I committed the sins of theft and murder. Now the highest judge of all, has worked his power upon me to ensure that I fully pay for them."

"How long do you need to remain as this?"

"Until my sentence is completed."

"How long is that?"

"I don't know. It's my fear that unless the good Lord decides to be merciful upon me and at last allow me entrance into his dominion that I'll be trapped in this manner in between worlds for as long as this place remains."

In response to this statement, Vanessa's Catholic upbringing took control of her once again and caused her to recall several of the lessons taught to her and her siblings when they were little by the priests of their childhood Catholic parish around the major Christian holidays. Those concerned spirits. Catholics believed that ghosts were the lingering spirits of the dead whose souls could not enter through the gates of heaven, as their souls were not at rest. Normally, this was caused by some unfinished business on Earth. They were fated to walk the Earth, but they were invisible to the mortal eyes because they were trapped within their own special realm, which existed in between the world of living and the world of the dead. It was called purgatory. Those ghosts remained there, until the issue was resolved allowing them to finally ascend into the hereafter.

However, there was also another reason souls ended up in purgatory, which was as a punishment for great sins committed in life. In this case, their presence in that nether world was a means of them paying penance for their previous actions in order to gain the forgiveness needed to make it possible for them to reside in heaven.

At once, every thing made sense. In the case of this ancient woman, her inability to enter heaven came from the sins she accumulated during her time on Earth. All of her adult years upon this Earth were in a command of pirate ship whose homeport was the Boston Harbor. She and her crew would have made their ill-gotten fortune through sailing down both the Boston River and the Charles River robbing ships of their goods, cargo, and seizing for themselves the possessions of the passengers and crew.

They would have also killed many who resisted. After her execution, the Almighty must have convened his own court to enforce his commandants through trying this female pirate for the sins of stealing and murder and worked his own divine will to ensure she bore the punishment for her actions.

There was one last inquiry, which Vanessa felt she must make of this ghostly woman. "How much more time do you have left," she probed. "I mean how much more time do you have left in which your spirit is visible?"

"My limited time in which the Lord allows me to interact and speak with the world of the living is fast passing. Soon, I'm afraid I'll be bared from this world again until tomorrow night."

"I'm sorry that you're trapped in this way."

"It's my own fault."

"Every one desires a chance at forgiveness, and a chance at a new beginning including those who have committed horrible crimes."

"I've brought this upon myself through the actions I committed in life and I must now bare the punishments for my sins so that one day he may forgive me and allow my spirit to pass through the gates of heaven."

"I hope the Lord forgives you and lets you into heaven."

"Why's that?"

"Everyone deserves a chance at forgiveness and redemption, no matter what crimes or mistakes they've committed in their life."

"Before tonight none to whom I've attempt to my make my presence know have sought to speak to me."

"Is there anything I can do?"

"Pray for my soul so the good Lord may yet be merciful upon me and end my sentence so I may know his love and be allowed entrance to his realm."

"How can I pray for you if I don't know your name?"

"I'm remembered not as Rena but only as the Murderess of the Harbor."

"I'll remember you."

"Thank for the kindness you've shown to me on this night."

"I'll pray for you, when I can."

"That is all I could ask."

Close to them, the street clock ticked signaling it was now just after ten. As if in response to the time, the light emanating from within the after image of the pirate woman, increased by several volumes before it began to dim. Vanessa assumed the woman's time on Earth was coming to its conclusion. It shimmered. A brief time passed before Vanessa saw that the apparition to whom she was just talking to only seconds ago was now gone. Once more, this pirate's soul was consigned to the purgatory in which she existed during the rest of the day.

Vanessa said a brief prayer for the woman. With that done, she at last entered the long sought goal of Boylston Station, inside of which she found the long sought sanctuary from both the storm and the spectral image that previously terrorized her. There she boarded an E Line train.

Soon she was back in the warmth of her apartment in the North End and after a quick shower, she felt the warmth and comfort that only Richard's strong arms could provide to her. They celebrated their anniversary.

Within a few days, Vanessa recovered from her terrible ordeal but she kept the spirit lady in her thoughts as she promised. She also prayed for her whenever possible.

However, from that day forward, Vanessa never again saw the ghostly pirate woman who was cursed to haunt Boston Commons, because now any time Vanessa needed to take the Green Line home to her blissfully wonderful domestic abode late at night she avoided Boston Commons by going straight to the Green Line Station at Boylston.

# Maternity Presents

Maria Flores Salazar stood by the hearth of the brownstone, which was located in the old quarter of the Martian city of Utopia Planitia and knew that on this evening she was alone. That was true. As her very tiny body leaned naturally to her left—she was born with scoliosis—Maria stretched upwards in her bright red high heels dusting the mantle place. She was born disabled. As she worked, her free hand rubbed her stomach and through the fabric of her bright red dress, she could feel the new lives that were now growing within her womb.

In her distracted state, she knocked a small case off the mantle place. Maria heard it crash land on the deck, breaking its side and letting its content spill out onto the deck plates. Maria knelt down to investigate finding framed photographs of her recently deceased mother were sprawled out at her feet. She sighed. Maria clutched the Catholic cross hanging around her neck and wished her mother was still alive so she could share in the joyous news she now possessed. She stood up.

Suddenly, Maria sensed an eerie and yet recognizable presence bear down upon her from behind as she also heard a familiar voice speak to her. "Hello, Maria," the voice called. "Hello, my child.

Maria recognized the voice at once because she heard it speak to her and her siblings all her life. She thought she imagined it. Her face briefly turned white due to a combination of shock and concern for the well being of the two precious cargo items, which she would be carrying for much of the next year. The voice repeated its message. Maria listened again and this time her mind confirmed her suspicions regarding the identity of the person. Her panic abated. A strong combination of great joy and great happiness spread through her very petite body in its place, which was accompanied by the light brown color returning to her face. That was her natural skin color. Very slowly, she turned herself around to face towards the front hatchway of the brownstone and found her now deceased mother, Anna Luna Flores, standing before her.

Maria smiled. "Hello, Mother," she said. "You look very well."

"Being dead does wonders to relive the body of the pain and ravages caused by cancer. How is your husband? Is he well?"

"He's very well mother, Devin's on his way home from the office at this very moment."

The Catholic cross shook on Maria's neck as she starred at her mother, or to be more precise her eyes were seeing through her mother's body because the older woman's body was that of a ghost. Anna Luna Flores—her husband was Marcus Flores—died nearly one year ago. The caused of her death was cancer. In the three years before her death, Anna fought a valiant but ultimately futile battle against the cancer that first appeared in her stomach before it spread to the rest of her body.

Anna studied her daughter. Although she looked down upon all of her children many times from heaven, which was where she now resided for all eternity, this was the first time she and Maria were together in the metaphorical flesh since her death. A cursory examination of her daughter's body indicated she gained weight in that time. It was concentrated on her stomach, her breasts, and her hips. Anna suspected she knew the cause and the bright light she noticed emanating from Maria's eyes as well as her face reinforced her suspicions but still, she desired confirmation from her daughter.

"You look very well, Maria," Anna stated. "In fact, you seem to be glowing."

"Yes, Mother, it's true."

"May I ask why?"

Maria was hesitant to answer. She ran her fingers very happily over her belly imagining all of the very wonderful changes that would be occurring to her over the next nine months. This morning she was given some very special news. It needed to be shared with her entire family but it was until now her intention that her husband would be the first to be informed of this excellent revelation. She smiled. The Almighty father and creator granted the wish she made earlier, after all only he possessed the power to let the dead speak with the living. Maria's plans changed

"I've got wonderful news, Mother," she revealed. "I'm pregnant, I'm pregnant for the first time, Mother!"

"Congratulations, Maria. I'm very happy for you,

Daughter," Anna Luna Flores responded. "Becoming a mother is a very momentous event in the life of any woman."

"Thank you, Mother," Maria cooed. "I can already feel how special it is. "

"You'll find the next nine months to be a very unique and also a very trying time for you, but it will be very rewarding."

"I know it will be so, Mother."

Maria was the youngest of five daughters. Marcus Flores, her father, taught religious history at one of the university's in the academic quarter of the Martian city that was Utopia Planitia. He was now retired. The city was constructed within a large sealed dome. All the cities, towns and settlements on Mars were construct inside of large reinforced domes, which was to protect the citizens of the city from the dangerous atmosphere of the red planet. Her mother worked as a librarian at one of the branches of the city's free library and retired when Maria was in high school. The ancestors on both sides of Maria's family line were devout Catholics. Her family's adherence to their faith stretched back over the previous generations to the first of Maria's forbears who migrated to Mars and it also went further backwards to Earth, in particularly to Spain, where her mother's ancestors came from, and Mexico, which was the country in which her father's distant ancestors resided in.

Marcus and Anna Flores brought up their daughters in their faith and raised them to be devoted good Catholic women. As part of that upbringing, all of their daughters were taught it was their obligation—no, it was their duty—to marry well and to have children. This ensured the continuation of humanity. It also ensured their family line would continue beyond the current generation, which were Maria and her four sisters.

All of Maria's older sisters, possessed families and they also possessed very successful careers in their respective fields. Maria did not want that. Instead, she wanted a life that was much more feminine and much more traditional for a woman. All she wanted her entire life was to be just a stay at home wife to a wonderful husband, which she already accomplished, and a stay at home mother. She wanted many children. Maria continued stroking her belly and could instinctually sense the stirring of the children that would be growing within her over the next year.

She peered ahead, finding the apparition of her mother's essence was moving closer to her. The movement did not make any noises. Maria starred ahead deducing that Anna's feet did not touch the deck plates as her entire body was instead floating over them. She took in her mother's ghostly form, which was blue and translucent and was surrounded by a projection of an outfit that the elder woman wore very often in life, which were a red and white checkered skirt and a pleated blouse. She recreated a pair of red high heels to wear on her feet.

Maria continued rubbing her belly. She was lost in thought feeling the emergence of the very special bond that could exist between a mother and her children when they were in her womb and knew it would became stronger as she carried them to term.

Tonight, she was very happy to share this magnificent news with her mother. Anna Luna Flores was already beginning to lose her battle against cancer, which spanned several years, when Devin asked Maria to become his bride. It was shortly after the wedding that Anna's health took a turn for the worst. She died last May. As grateful as she was for this magnificent opportunity Maria knew she was only confided part of that news of the momentous events that alter the course of her life. "Mother, I'm have more news," she admitted. "I'm with more than one child."

"Are you going to have triplets?"

"I wish I was, Mother, but I'm not."

"How many are you having?"

"Twins, Mother, my first pregnancy is twins."

"I'm very happy for you Maria."

"Oh Mother, I've been dreaming of this since I was a little girl."

"I know."

"I can't wait to experience all of the physical changes all of my older sisters went through before me when they were pregnant with their first child and I am certain Devin will enjoy watching them occur."

"He will, men normally enjoy that part of their wife becoming pregnant the most."

"I'll being enjoying it even more than he will, Mother"

"Have you told your husband of this?"

"I've not been able to yet, Mother. The doctor told me the news this morning," Maria answered. "I will tell Devin when he comes home tonight."

"Have you thought of any name for them?"

"I've picked out a few names, Mother. Since I'm hoping they're both girls I want to name them Anna and Jeanette to honor you and grandmom and give life back to the two of you through doing so."

A loud chime came front hatchway, which indicated that someone was at the door, and it's sounding interrupted the very tender conversation between mother and daughter. Maria's heart warmed. She hoped her husband was home from the office. It was followed by a loud buzz, which meant the outer hatch was opening to allow a person access to the front airlock of the Martian habitat. Maria patted her belly. A long and very wonderful smile formed on her face because as she was still the only living person in the living room that meant her husband was home. Her heart skipped a beat.

Anna Luna Flores heard the audio signals also but before she could speak her image flickered. Maria saw it. Her heart sank because it was a sign that her mother's presence here would be ending soon. "Go to your husband," Anna Luna commanded. "It's time for you to inform him that you're pregnant."

"Mother, I want to spend more time with you before you disappear."

"Don't worry my child, I'll still be here when you're done. Now go to your husband and tell him your news."

"Yes Mother, you're right."

Maria reached up to her topknot removing the tie, which held her bright red hair in place and then untied the topknot she tied her hair into this morning. Her hair cascaded down her shoulders. She ran her fingers over light pink housedress smoothing out the few wrinkles she found ensuring she look the best for her husband but did adjust the apron that hung around her waist instead of removing it. The tie was stowed into one of pockets on it.

She started forward. Maria passed through apparition of

her recently deceased mother, which made it possible for her to feel both her mother's soul and the love her mother possessed for her. In just a second, she was on the other side. Her hair shook behind her and the hoop earrings she was wearing bounced in her ear lobes as she sauntered to the front hatchway. The inner hatch opened. Maria darted very fast and sensually on her heels reaching the hatch a few seconds before her husband came inside the habit. She flashed Devin a big smile. "Hello my darling," Maria purred. "Welcome home."

Anna Luna Flores remained behind. Although, she was only hear as a spirit, it was still possible for her to observe the actions of both Devin and Maria and could hear them exchange greetings with each other from behind her. On the other hand, Devin could only sense his mother in law's presence but he could neither see her the representation of her soul nor hear her voice. Tonight Anna's incorporeal being was visible only to Maria and only she could hear her voice. That was on purpose. It was Maria who wished to share the news of her pregnancy with her mother, and that was why the Almighty allowed Anna to briefly descend from the heavens above to perform her visit. As what passed for Anna's body floated there, she became curious as to what was occurring behind her and so her thoughts command her essence to spin around over the deck. Now she pointed herself towards the front hatchway so she could take in the sight of her daughter and her husband embracing each other. At present, Devin was stroking Maria's cheek.

"Devin, I've got some truly wonderful and magnificent to confine to you tonight," Maria cooed. "I'm pregnant and I'm pregnant with twins."

Devin kissed his wife's cheek. "That is such wonder news," he responded. "These will be just the first of the many children we will have tighter."

"I love that Devin, that's just how I want it."

"Have you eaten dinner yet?"

"The dinner is prepared but I haven't eaten yet, I was waiting for you to come home to eat."

Devin stroked his wife's cheeks. As he heard her purr softly, he studied her expression, which informed her that Maria was deep in her thought. She wanted to be alone. "You seem to want to spend more time in privacy with your imminent motherhood."

"I do."

"'I'll give you sometime alone with your thoughts and your dreams."

"Thank you, husband."

"I'll go and set the table and prepare it to be served."

"Call me when dinner is on the table."

Devin kissed her, which made her swoon in desire. He left for the kitchen. Once he was gone, Maria looked over her shoulders observing the apparition of her mother was still present behind her. Anna's body flickered again. Maria knew her tender visit with her mother must be almost over. Still she desired to spend as much time with the deceased matriarch of the Flores clan before she returned to the white clouds that comprised her new heavenly home and to that end, her high heels led her back to her mother.

Anna hovered in place watching her very proud daughter conduct her return trip to the spot in front of the hearth. Her ghostly pair of eyes made it possible to deduce the smile from earlier was still present on her daughter's lips and it was now not only wider than earlier but was also shinning brightly. She starred closer. The great radiant light that came from Maria's cheeks shone ahead making it seem that even Anna's light blue silhouette was gold. It was obvious to both women that the same was true in her eyes, which were normally dark black but right now, they resembled bright diamonds. Maria came to her mother. While her hair flapped behind her body, her heels ended her movement and kept from going back through the familiar spirit she very much missed over the past year.

"Oh Mother," Marie hummed. "This feels better than I could've ever imagined

"This is something you always wanted."

"It's so, Mother, I've been dreaming of this day since I was a little girl."

"You will be a wonderful mother."

Before she could say any more the projection of Anna Luna Flores flickered for the third time. This occurrence disturbed both mother and daughter because this time some of Anna's color briefly faded away. Her projection vanished for a brief second. Maria was very upset their reunion was at is end and considered protesting her mother's immediate disappearance. She did not for it would accomplish nothing. Maria knew that her mother now lived in a different plane of existence, which prevented her from remaining indefinitely upon this Earth.

Maria closed her lips. The Almighty granted the wish she made earlier and in doing so he allowed Anna Luna Flores to not only share in the happiness of her daughter's news that she was pregnant but also allowed the proud Flores matriarch to be present when the magnificent news was shared with the husband of her youngest daughter. To Maria that was enough. "I must be going," Anna admitted. "I must return from whence I came."

"I understand, Mother," Maria admitted. "I miss you and my grand parents greatly."

"I will see you again when you have also passed beyond the mortal realm and have entered the kingdom of heaven."

"I hope its not that long mother to wait before we are reunited."

"There's a chance I'll be able to convince the Almighty to let me descend to witness the birth of your first two children."

"I'll be praying and wishing for that, Mother."

"My grandchild will find themselves very fortunate to have you as their mother."

Maria blushed at the sentiment, as this was indeed high praise. Anna Luna Flores moved closer to her daughter, because she desired to hold Maria one last time in a warm familial embrace and spread her arms out to her tight to her. Maria stepped forward in her high heels. She was consumed with a desire to hug her mother one last time before Anna returned to the heavenly realm of the Almighty. She stopped. As Maria's eyes starred through her mother, her arms came up because she sought to wrap them around the free floating vapor, which contained Anna's essence in a tight feminine hug.

Mother and daughter respectively stood and floated in place. They embraced each other. At least that was would have happened if were both still living beings, since Anna was the half of the pair that was not composed of flesh and blood, her arms went through Maria's upper body making contact with her soul. Maria stepped forward further. Her body passed through her mother's essence, which resulted in her feeling as if her mother managed to be both inside of her and around her at once.

Anna smiled. She knew that she and Marcus not only succeeded in their efforts to raise their daughter to be a good Catholic woman but that their family line would continue beyond the younger generation that was their five daughters. Maria felt at ease. From where she remained, she very briefly wobbled in her high heels, in response to the warmth of her mother's spirit washing over her, which contained within in it a mixture of both great concern and the depth of her mother's love for her. That did not summon it up well enough. Contained with it was her mother's affection for not only the rest of her family but also her devotion to the two unborn children growing within Maria's womb, whom marked the start of her own little branch of the Salazar clan.

Then she felt something else. It was a nonlocalized phenomenon, whose origin could not be determine, which was several times more powerful but it seemed to come from somewhere that was located beyond time and beyond space. This force was buried underneath the specter of her mother. In addition, it was very old and if Maria were to guess its age, she would say it was very ancient because it felt as if it pre dated not only humanity but also the entire universe.

At first Maria, could not identity it. As it came into contact with her mortal being she was terrified that her soul and everything that comprised her own person identity would be consumed by this archaic force but her alarm was unwarranted for as it passed through her body she could sense a great compassion and a great tenderness that brought joy to her eyes.

All her life she knew of the existence of this power for her parents and her childhood priests in her childhood parish taught about its love, it's teaching and its commandments. There were moments in the past when she could briefly sense it. It was not until this very moment in time that she could truly sense it or the vast stretch of its power and she did Maria knew instantly its identity. It was the Almighty father.

"Mother, I've got a request to make before you leave," Maria whispered. "Give my best to my grandparents when you see them again."

"I will, my daughter," Anna Luna responded. "I love you my daughter, you'll make a wonderful mother to my grandchild."

"I love you, Mother, and thank you, I've got a wonderful role model that I was the devoted student of as a child."

Following that statement Maria saw her mother's protection of her core conscious flicker again. It signaled her visit reached its conclusion. The color faded away. Maria fought back tears of great sadness as she watched the astral from of Anna Luna Flores dematerialize before it disappeared leaving her alone in the spot where mother once floated.

As Maria stood before the hearth of the dwelling in her high heels, she found that she very nearly cried out of the brief fear that her mother's soul was gone forever more. Her smile vanished. Then as she stood there, with her eyes starring around the living room, Maria's thoughts from earlier returned to her.

Her eyes tilted down to her belly imaging how wonderfully round and plumb it would be in nine months time, which was when she on the verge of giving birth, and she stroked her stomach again. She purred.

She could still feel her mother's presence. It was no longer located within the confines of the Martian residence. Instead, it came from that heavenly realms, that existed beyond time and beyond space from, which all human souls came from and from which they all returned to after death.

Anna Luna Flores died. In doing so vacated the role of matriarch, which was currently occupied by Maria's oldest sister, but it was certain the former matriarch would in death continue her duties by looking down to watch over all of Anna's family including the two unborn twins Maria carried within her womb. Maria's smile broadened.

A masculine voice shouted from the kitchen, which filled her with warmth again because it was her husband getting her attention. "Maria," Devin called. "Dinner's on the table, come and get it while it's hot."

"Thank you, handsome," Maria replied, "I'm coming and I'll be there soon."

She spun in her high heels, the points and tips of her high heels hitting the deck beneath her as she made her way into the kitchen. In a few moments time, Maria found herself approaching the kitchen table where her husband was waiting for her with his open wide. She approached him. Before she could speak, Devin wrapped his strong masculine hands around Maria's arm and pulled her close to him for an embrace. She bounced in her high heels. Her heart was racing out of a lovely combination of passion and desire as her body close to her husband and their flesh rubbed together under the their clothes. Devin leaned down to kiss her red lips. "I love you, my wonderful wife," he whispered. "And our unborn children."

"Devin, I'll give you all the children you could ever want."

"I know you'll do so."

"Devin, I've been thinking of names for our children," she admitted. "If they are girls we should call them Anna and Jeannette."

"Both of those will be wonderful names for our daughters," Devin responded. "What shall we call them if they're sons?"

"Why, Jonathan and Fredrick, after your father and your own grandfather."

"That's an excellent idea."

Maria returned the earlier romantic gesture by planting a big kiss on her husband's lips, as she rubbed her soon to be swollen belly against Devin's muscular and well-toned stomach. Her husband stroked her red hair. As she stood in her high heels, Maria titled her head up however slightly letting the wonderfully strong gaze from her husband's eyes, fall down on her, which filled her with glee before she put her head on his chest. She hummed blissfully.

"I know what we'll named them if our twins are one son and one girl," Devin declared. "We'll name them Anna and Jonathan to give life back to your mother and my father."

"I love that Devin, that's such a wonderful idea."

# Spring Break Date

It was a very warm and beautiful Jovian Spring day.
"I wish this doesn't end," Penelope Galanis Turner muttered, "I hope it never ends."

Her boyfriend and future husband did not hear her words because Penelope said them so very softly under her breath, which made it hard for her own ears to detect them as her head rested on the shoulder of her handsome suitor. His name was Joseph Bernoulli. On this Sunday in March, they made their way down Hudson Boulevard, as they were celebrating Joseph's return to their hometown from college this week. He was on his spring break. Penelope struggled to suppress the strong feelings of excitement, which very warmly coursed through her mind and body. They walked ahead. As her high heels touched the pavement, Penelope's desires clarified themselves because she knew now it was not the day but all the wonder that she felt from being in Joseph's arms that she wanted to continue forever.

Her bright brown eyes starred ahead. "Do we have to go to this clearance sale today, Penelope?" she heard Joseph inquire.

"You said you wanted to go out this weekend," Penelope replied. "That's what we're doing today Joe, we're going out to this sale together, and then we're going out again this evening after you pick me up to take me out when we go to dinner and the movies."

The young couple's hometown was named Mountainside. It was one of the human settlements located in Prospect County on the moon of Io, which itself was the fourth moon of Jupiter. Mountainside was created as a farming community. It and the other towns and settlements surrounding it were established centuries ago as agricultural settlements, which was back when humans were just beginning to create the initial colonies and outposts on the various moons orbiting Jupiter and Saturn. In time that changed. It was after the lines for the core shuttles and the transit shuttle tubes were extended outwards from Pioneer City, the local metropolis, to Mountainside connecting it to the city and the other towns.

Today, Mountainside was a small suburban town. The lifeblood of its economy was not devoted only to industry or manufacturing but was instead both of those two combined. Many farmers still resided in the town. In addition, throughout the town there was a thriving range of small and independent businesses, which were owned by the town's residents.

That made it something else instead, something special.

In fact, it was as unique as Penelope was. She wanted to not only marry Joseph and have his children but also wanted to have a career in academia, as a scholar of literature and poetry for those were the subjects she was majoring in. Joseph shifted his head slightly and leaned over planting a small peck on her brow. "You're a very pleasant sight for my eyes, which are tired after my midterms," Joseph said. "I just didn't think our date would involve me taking my gal to a discount clothing sale."

Penelope moaned. She was very happy to again see the man she was going to marry again because they did not have much time for each other over the last two weeks. Early March was always the time for spring midterms. Recently her only contact with Joseph consisted of brief late conversations conducted on the video link, the dedicated communications console, after they finished their course work for the day. That was not enough. Although Penelope enjoyed the erotic thrill of their late night and clandestine communications, she still lived at home; it was not the same as being with him in the flesh.

Today, she could feel not only his powerful gaze upon her lovely young body but also sense his breath upon her skin. This was what she was craving since their last date. She smiled.

"It's not a clearance sale or a discount clothing sale, Joe," she muttered. "It's a rummage sale."

"What's the difference?"

"At the first two you can only buy clothes, but a rummage sale has much more beyond outfits."

Penelope's right arm was tightly wrapped around Joseph's left arm and his fingers were tightly clasped around her own arm, which was an artificial one. This limb was the product of an old injury. Years ago on a Girl Scout canoe trip her canoe capsized and in doing so crushed the right arm she was born with requiring it to be amputated at the nearest hospital and replaced with a prosthetic. The strap of her Catholic cross, which was the symbol of the faith of her father, Galerius, bounced on its strap around her neck. With it, she wore a veil. This was a representation of her mother Diana's Greek ancestry. It also symbolized Diana Turner's ancestry as part of the Greek orthodox, which she was born into it. She converted to Catholicism before marrying Penelope's father. As she moved in her high heels, Penelope could feel the veil rub against the shoulder straps of her dress.

Her high resting ponytail shook behind her head. Penelope's hoop earrings jingled in response to her movement. She was letting Joseph lead her towards the local Baptist church, which hosted the rummage sale they were going to today, and it was located only a little beyond their old high school. "What other things do they sell there?" Joseph asked.

"Many things such as decorations, books, classics movie discs and music discs, shoes, furniture. In fact it has everything a young couple needs to create a home and a life together."

"First we need a home and to be married."

"We'll need to live together first."

"Your parents will not allow us to advance our courtship or wed right now."

"According to both the law and the tenants of our faith, I'm old enough to legally marry or live with anyone I want."

"Remember the terms of our courtship that your parents negotiated with mine."

"I know, I know we can't wed until or live together as a couple until after I've turned twenty one."

"They feel us doing either until you are that age is inappropriate."

"I'll be twenty one in a few months, Joe."

"Yes, that's true."

"After my birthday, there's nothing my parents our yours can do to prevent us."

"I very much look forward to that."

"As do I, Joe."

As they walked, Penelope felt the strong feelings escalating within her and they all most tempted her into falling into a nice little walking sleep on her fiancé's arm. She first recognized them several hours ago when Joseph picked her up this morning after breakfast but for the last few hours, she was able to suppress them. It was getting harder to do so. This morning for the first stage of their date, the two went to the weekly Sunday morning mass at the local Catholic Church. After that, they walked into the downtown village. There they ate brunch at the local dinner, Joseph paid for their meal and their coffee, and afterwards they passed through the town park on their walk to Prospect Boulevard.

Joseph ran his hand along the top of Penelope's hair. The action made her grin. It also produced a little moan from her, which reflected how strong her desires were becoming at this point. Still she resisted surrendering to them. However, she was not certain how much longer she could do so, which caused Penelope's internal defenses came online at once and very hastily constructed a very thick wall around her higher brain functions to protect them so she could continue to remain in full control of her body. At least for now.

As Penelope looked at him, Joseph stroked her chin. "I've been thinking," he admitted. "At the end of this academic term we should rent a small private apartment together, which is located off campus."

"I'm looking forward to it, thank you for taking me to this rummage sale."

"It's a great chance to finally be with my bride to be."

Penelope's body warmed at the compliment. "Thank you Joseph, I'm sure I'll even be able to find something nice at this sale to wear when I come to campus to visit you next."

"When will that be?"

"Next weekend to celebrate my being done with the last of my midterm papers."

"You'll look lovely in whatever you select."

"Thank you Joseph, I'm certain you'll enjoy this sale."

"Perhaps, tell me Penelope, how do you learn about this rummage sale?"

"Oh, I don't want to tell but I've got my sources."

She smiled dainty at Joseph.

In truth, that was a little white lie. Today would be Penelope's second time going to the sale because she visited it last year. This was last year when her older sister, Athena, was visiting with her husband and during that stay Athena, Penelope and their mother decided to leave the Turner residence. They walked up to the rummage sale. On that trip, Penelope brought a few lovely dresses, and a few skirts using the money she earned from her part time work at the local bridal shop. That included her current dress.

Penelope inhaled and smelled the flowers, which they passed on their stroll all of which were in bloom. She sighed.

"Is something wrong?" Joseph inquired.

"I just wish we're walking somewhere on a nice beach or

a nice garden where there was a nice breeze and a nice wind blowing on us."

"That's the downside of living in a dome."

"Yes, Joe, I understand."

The enclosure surrounding their town was necessary. Io possessed a very thin atmosphere. In fact, it was even thinner than the air contained within the high peaks of the many mountainous regions on humanity's ancestral home world of Earth. Alas, all of this was a product of the moon's atmosphere being stripped away courtesy of the strong pull, which was naturally exerted upon it by the massive magnetic field generated, by Jupiter.

In addition, humans could not breathe the air. The major element in the atmosphere outside the domes and the other forms of enclosures, which were littered across the surface of the moon, was sulfur dioxide. It was deadly to humans. This was a product of the mass number of active volcanoes plus the large ring of charged particles spread through the upper atmosphere. All of that considered the day felt wonderful.

Penelope partially closed her eyes. She let her imagination run wild and pretended a nice small breeze was hitting her dress as the legs of it, a product of the long split going down the side to her ankles, swung hither and yonder rubbing against her light olive flesh. It was delightful. Her eyes peered up at her boyfriend and she rapidly moved her eyelids, which were bright pink because she coated them in that color eye shadow, she was batting them to silently tease her soon to be husband.

"You've convinced me, my sweet," Joseph spoke. "I'll enjoy seeing this rummage sale and taking you to it."

"Really, Joe? You mean it?"

"I do."

"I knew you would enjoy it."

Joseph put his fingers under Penelope's chin, titled it up slightly, turning it towards his own face. "It's worth it all to see you and to see you in such a wonderful outfit."

He kissed her lips.

Penelope whimpered. At once, she knew this was missed the most about being with him and that was how marvelous his touch felt. Joseph's eyes bore down on her. All of the sensations were becoming stronger and they threatened to overwhelm her.

"Joseph, today has been so wonderful," Penelope hummed. "Mass and the brunch were delightful."

"You're most welcome."

Joseph leaned closed and kissed her pink lips again. She returned the kiss. Her suitor pulled back but despite his action, Penelope detected very strong vibrations running through her as if her whole body was trembling in pleasure. Penelope knew why. It was certain any embrace between them would never be anything but wonderful for Joseph would never violate her or abuse her trust. After all, he won her heart. In only a matter of time, they would be man and wife.

Feeling Joseph's imposing stare as he discreetly admired Penelope in her lovely long green dress was so strong that the wall blocking her intense passions was in danger of collapsing. "Joseph," Penelope gushed, "I've always felt it was very special that you chose to go to a university so close to home."

"I didn't want our courtship to be a long distance one."

"That's one of the many reasons why I'm going to marry you Joseph Bernoulli."

"Remind me of the name of the church to which we're going for this sale."

"It's the Reformed Armory Church."

"Isn't that the name of the Baptist church that's located down by Mountainside High School, my lovely little Mrs. Joseph Bernoulli?"

"It is, I can't wait for that to be my last name."

"All in good time Penelope, then you will truly be Mrs. Joseph Bernoulli."

"Mrs. Joseph Bernoulli," Trisha muttered. "Mrs. Joseph Bernoulli. I'm Mrs. Joseph Bernoulli and this is my husband."

Saying those words felt magical.

They did more to Penelope's mind than she could have imagined. All of the immense cravings combined themselves and prepared for an all out assault against Penelope's mental defenses. She felt overwhelmed. Inside of her, she knew her mental barriers were struggling to absorb and withstand the blasts fired by her needs, but despite the valiant resistance, a large hole was blasted in her protective emotional shields. Shortly afterwards they collapsed. With her emotional core and her mental processing unit exposed, her accumulated desires seeped in and wave after wave of pure desire washed over her.

"Mrs. Joseph Bernoulli," she moaned, "I'm going to soon be Mrs. Joseph Bernoulli."

Joseph heard her. As she pushed her head deep in his shoulder, he looked at her in concern. "Penelope, is something wrong?"

"Oh nothing's wrong dear," she whimpered, "I'm just thinking of what it'll be like once we're are finally married."

Penelope partially closed her eyes. She barely noticed the people who passed them because to her time seemed to be slowing down as if her mind was taking a photograph of the events occurring on the street to preserve them forever in her memory. Yet again she said what her, married name would be. This time it acted as a hypnotic trigger and at once, it deactivated the remnants and the shambles of her protections. She hummed. Now her desires were in full control of her mind and body, which at last let Penelope, understand why they were accumulating over the last two weeks because during all those nights of speaking on the vid links her passions for her suitors' physical presence were left unfilled.

Uncapped cravings flowed uncontrolled through her essence.

In response, the higher functions of Penelope's brain deactivated themselves and her consciousness retreated inwards where it settled into a warm bed comprised of her own red hot emotions. Only automatic functions were maintained. She transfer all navigational control and full control of the steering of her body over to Joseph and his strong arm, because she trusted him to not betray her trust or abuse her, for the remaining time that she would be coupled to his arm. Her core consciousness was other wise occupied. Right now, it was enjoying the overwhelming waves of happiness that coursed through her.

They lit a fire within her.

Penelope's flesh tingled. Her body shuddered slightly in her high heels as she sank deeper into the delightful trance because within her brain there currently only existed thoughts of her and Joseph, their courtship, there relationship, their eventually marriage. Her mind was now in standby mode. If it needed to for some reason, it would arise again to retake control of her movement from her boyfriend.

Then she felt it.

A great power was flowing from Joseph through his arm and out from his hand and into her spirit along with her body, which made Penelope's face beam as her eyes partially closed. This was a familiar energy. It symbolized not only the strong emotional bond between them but also the strong spiritual bond, which always reminded her that Joseph was the man for her and the one whom she would be with to the end of her life. In time, she would be his wife. Soon she would return that love not only with devotion but also in time with children. The magical words that would be her married name still danced through her mind and this time they did so with a number.

Three.

That was it. It was a number, which Penelope thought of often. To her it was a very magical one, not only because of the holy trinity of the religion to which she, her suitor, her parents and her future in laws belonged to but also because of a more personal reason. That was the length of her and Joseph's courtship.

Then something truly unusual occurred.

Penelope's spirit seemed to leave her body and mind as it traveled in time. It threw itself backwards three years to the start of her blissful romantic courtship, which put her back in high school. Penelope attended Mountainside High School. That was the local high school, and in her junior year of high school, she selected Ancient Earth Literature for her required English class for that year. Joseph was one of the students in her class. They met on the first day of that term and Penelope feel in love at Joseph at once thinking him to be most handsome, in particular, since he was a year older.

A few months later, he asked her out for the first time. On their first date, he escorted her to the fall dance hosted by Mountain Side High School and following the wonderful time she experienced at the dance, they continued going out. In December of that year, Joseph asked Penelope if he could take her to the holiday party hosted by the local Catholic Church. Both of their families attended it. That night as he walked her back to the Turner family residence Joseph informed Penelope of his desire to marry and have a family with a good Catholic woman. To her massive delight and surprise, he also informed her that he desired her to be her wife.

Without any fear or hesitation, Penelope accepted the offer. Once their respective parents approved their courtship began with the understanding they could not be married or reside together as a couple before Penelope turned twenty-one. As it proceeded, he constantly romanced her. In turn, she provided plenty of feminine allure to not just impress on their dates but also enamor him through intrigue and physical seduction. Come the end of the year, Joseph graduated. He went off to one of the local universities, Hudson University, which was located in the neighboring town of Pine Ville, to study engineering. Their courtship continued. Following her own high school graduation, Penelope chose to attend the same university returning the romantic gesture her betrothed made the year before but lived at home to save up money for their eventual married life.

Penelope's consciousness was thrown forward in time.

She did not come back to the moment her mind first left her body but instead continued traveling and journeyed further into the future. Her spirit came to inhabit the local church. As she floated close to the ceiling, she peered down and watched her father as he walked her slightly older self down the aisle to Joseph. She saw herself becoming his bride. Penelope noticed her body was dressed in a lovely white dress that was similar to one of bridal dresses contained at the bridal store at which she worked. It looked beautiful on her.

Her mind resumed its travels. Penelope felt her very essence travel down the course of her and Joseph's life and saw their destiny, which was to spend their life together as man and wife. She observed them. In the future, she could tell despite their financial status might be or the would be very happy together life together. Joseph began a career as an engineer. It prospered. So did her career as a literary scholar but they never stopped loving each other or being committed to each other.

She saw her body change getting rounder, fuller and curvier.

That was from the children that were yet to come. Penelope monitored her future self. She become pregnant several times and give several children to Joseph and saw in total, the number she saw was four. Two boys and the remaining two were girls. Each time Penelope also glimpsed how eager she and Joseph were at the prospect of welcoming another little one into their family.

A person spoke. It was very far away but also very loving.

It was Joseph's voice and he was summoning her back to him. Penelope giggled. Her being came rushing back to the present moment in time and her psyche rose out of the warm sleep. Her eyes lit up. Once more, her mind arose and it mentally stretched out through her walking form taking back control of her body's movement and her navigation. "Penelope," Joseph said. "Penelope, my dear."

"Yes, Joseph?"

"We're here at the church if this is the rummage sale."

Penelope opened her eyes all the way. She investigated their surroundings and found in front of them was a white building with a tall steeple, the church, and a smaller building across from it, which was the rectory. In it the priests lived. On the front lawn were a few long white lawn tables covered by cloths and a few bright blue tarps, which spread out around them on which goods were displayed to be sold by the volunteers running the rummage sale.

"No, Joseph," Penelope explained. "This is it."

"It doesn't look like much."

"It's the sale."

Joseph released his grip on his betrothed's arm. Since Penelope's mind was back in full control of her the steering of her body, she was able to easily take control of her movements. Her head rose. She detached her arm from its place around her future husband's arm. "Enjoy the sale, darling," Penelope muttered. "I'm going to go shopping."

Penelope gave her suitor a little parting peak on his cheek and then she departed walking forwards in her high heels, which caused her hoop earrings to shake and made the legs of her dress sway in a most alluring and seductive manner. Her purse swung. She came to the closest tarp on which she kneeled down on it and busied herself with examining the collection of skirts, blouses, dresses and other items of women's clothing, which were all spread out on it. Joseph she knew was moving among the tables comprising the sale. Penelope turned her head around. She peered over her shoulder and noticed Joseph pause at one of the tables on top of it were displayed a mixture of used hardcover books and a mixture of used paperback books. Her attention went back to the collection. She selected two beautiful long dresses, which were the ones she liked the most and picked them up to decide which of them to buy. Her eyes checked the tags, ensuring they were the right size to fit her. She checked the price tags. To her immense delight, both only cost only one Jovian credit and so she decided to buy both, which gave her one dress for the movies tonight and one for her visit to Joseph next weekend.

Penelope stood up. She looked behind her and discovered Josephs stood at the center table because that was the one at which the cast register was located. Penelope began to move. Her high heels passed over the freshly mowed spring grass and crushed some under the weight of her high heels as she walked to join Joseph at the center table. Soon she came up to her soon to be husband.

A clerk handed Joseph a bag. He peered over his shoulder

and the saw the woman he wanted to grow old with stopping right beside him "Did you find any nice outfits here today Penelope?" he asked.

Penelope stopped at his side. "I did," she answered. "I think they'll be very lovely on me."

She paid for her new outfits. Joseph moved off, as he already paid for the books he decided to buy and Penelope followed coming close to his body. His arm went out. She was offering it to him just as he did when he came to pick her up to take her to mass this morning. The sight filled Penelope with glee. She wrapped her arm around on Joseph's shoulder.

"Today was wonderful, Joe," Penelope confessed. "I can't wait to go to the movies but I'm glad its tonight."

"Why's that?"

"My feet are sore from dwalking in my heels."

"You'll have plenty of time to rest your feet, once I've gotten you home."

"That's true, I can't wait to come back to the sale next year."

"I'll take you to it, we'll make it an annual tradition."

That pleased Penelope greatly. Joseph guided her down Hudson Boulevard in the direction from which they came taking his bride to be home. Penelope hummed. She was very happily recreating her pose from earlier. As the young couple moved ahead the feelings from earlier returned and Penelope once more turned directional control of her body over to her husband to be and let her mind once more descend into the very happy trance like state it was in earlier.

# Ghostly Street Train

It was very early in the morning. As Jennifer Taylor stood within the Astor Place subway station, located in the borough of Manhattan, and waited for her morning train, she felt her young body tremble in fear whilst the sides of her bright pink hijab rubbed against her light brown skin. She knew the cause of her great terror. It was the translucent subway engine. At this very moment, it was currently rolling into the New York subway station, which meant it was also coming directly towards where she stood on the platform.

"No," Jennifer cried. "That can't be so. That's not my morning subway train."

From the platform, she again detected the eerie sound of a horn blowing. She remained there. Once again her ears registered the presence of the very unusual audio vibrations, which first alerted her to the existence of this phantom sight and those were the horrifying ways in which several round objects screeched as they not only spun atop the subway tracks but also passed through them. That was a few minutes ago. In response, Jennifer peered into the distance and saw strange lights coming from within the darkness of the tunnel.

Right now, those same lights bore down upon Jennifer. In response to it, Jennifer lost her balance in her high heels and stumbled backwards over the cold concrete of the platform. Her hijab whacked against her cheeks. As she sought to regain her balance in her shoes, her long black traditional Muslim dress rubbed against the unnatural curve in her back because she was born with scoliosis. In Jennifer's case, it was not severe. In addition, her disability would not show up on anything except an x-ray, which was performed at the doctor's office or a scan that was conducted with a magnetic resonance imaging scanner at the hospital.

Jennifer did not move far. After she passed just a few inches from where she previously stood she was able to get her legs to stop and regain her balance so she once more she stood motionless.

"Escape," Jennifer muttered. "That's what's needed. I've got to escape. I've got to get away from here and this ghost train. Another train. That's what I'll do, I'll catch a subway train at the next station to the store at 42nd Street. I may be a bit late getting to work today but with the terrible shape that the metro system is in right now no one at work including the managers will not be at all that surprised when I tell them I was delayed due to trouble with the subway system."

Jennifer tried to move. Alas, to her great distress she discovered she could not execute her plan because her body was still frozen in place out of sheer terror. The immaterial engine advanced on her. Now with her peering eyes she could see that something was coupled to the rear of it.

Jennifer studied it.

It was long. In addition, it was immaterial. Underneath, it there was a set of equally translucent wheels. The shape was rectangular. It was not solid.

From Jennifer's very brief and equally frightful observations, she could deduce that it was flickering in and out of existence. Furthermore, it was not made of metal. As she tried to find protection from the danger and calm her emotions in her devotion to her Muslim faith, Jennifer came to accept it would be better to describe this object as being composed of a mixture of vapors and trailing smoke. To her confusion, it still managed to possess some slight physical presence. Within the middle of it, there was a door. Also Jennifer could deduce that located very close to the ceiling were a set windows, which were composed of a thin smoky texture.

A ghostly rail car speed towards her.

"It's not real!" Jennifer shouted. "It doesn't exist, it can't be so, no train on the New York subway station looks the way this one does," she gripped her hijab, "Allah, Allah protect me."

She recited the muslin prayer for protection.

Her fingers, firmly gripped the sides of the symbol of her faith. Jennifer saw that this most unusual train stopped at the platform and her eyes glared at it. Her blood raced. The proximately of these two mysterious objects to her being greatly increased her existing fear and in front of her the door opened. She starred inside it. Suddenly, Jennifer swore she heard music playing from somewhere in the station but from where she was not certain. In caused her to become even more fearful and since she was concerned it originated on the platform she decided to very warily step inside the carriage in desperation because she was seeking to escape the dreaded instrumental arrangement.

She got a few feet within the vehicle and there her eyes scanned the interiors.

"This isn't right," Jennifer whispered, "this definitely isn't my normal train. I don't think this train exists on any branch of the New York subway system in Manhattan or the rest of the city. Correction. I know it doesn't exist on the subway system."

Around her, she saw no rows of orange seats. Instead, she saw many leather couches that were located along the walls, which were black in color and in front of them, were several black leather armchairs. In the center, she saw a group of brown armchairs that were arranged in a circle. All of them glowed before her eyes. There was something very strange and peculiar about this subway car and then once more she felt her body terminate all movement because it turned as rigid as if she were an ice sculpture. This time it was not alone. Her mind did the same as she detected more of the orchestral melody, which was now even louder than before and was to her great distress coming from somewhere close to her.

She listened to it.

Her limbs trembled.

Her heart pounded.

It was because she realized as the music continued to play that it came from within the confines of this very strange vehicle. Jennifer's heart beat rapidly. While her hijab continued to dangle around her face, she traced the orchestral sound back to its source, which she concluded was a table in the middle of the circle she spotted earlier. Upon it, sat an ancient phonograph.

Jennifer discovered her dark black eyes could move but only barely, which allowed her to perform another quick scan off her surroundings and in the distance she discovered a stove. That could not be possible. There were no stoves in any subway car or in any train but then she became greatly alarmed, as she smelled something.

Soon she recognized the flavor.

To Jennifer's great horror, it was meat.

Her skin crawled.

Since it's mere presence could not only potentially violate the dietary restrictions of her faith but also because from the way it smelled it was as if something was being cooked. There was no point to Jennifer trying to determine what meal was being prepared within the oven.

It was then her voice broke. "This is not any normal subway car," she uttered, "I've got to get out of here and I've got to do so at once before something else happens to me that's even worse than this."

Despite her determination, her body would not comply.

It was there Jennifer remained.

She fought through her fears.

It took seconds.

At last, she could move.

Her high heels shifted.

Now that she was back in control of her body, Jennifer forced herself to move backwards, which made her purse swing on her shoulders and made her hijab dangle as she sought to preserve her very life. Her high heels clicked together. Soon she arrived at the car doors, which were thankfully still open. This enabled her to continue her flight because she would not allow herself to cease her reverse momentum right now as the instrumental arrangement was at its loudest.

Jennifer's heart pounded. "I can't stop," she said. "I've got to get out of here before any more specters appear."

She summoned up her courage.

In addition, she did not turn herself around. That would take time she did not have and so she went through the doors the way she was with her chest facing towards the interior of the coach. Her attention was fixated ahead. In seconds, she emerged onto the platform but her mind decided she could not stop her reverse motion. She continued going backwards. Soon she was even further away from the phantom train and it was only then that Jennifer did finally halt.

She studied the engine.

There was no number 6 on it.

In front of her the engine shimmered and so did its one lonesome car before both vanished from the tracks.

Jennifer looked out on the tracks. Once more, the station was deserted with the exception of Jennifer whose lungs were still panting in anxiety. Seconds later, her skin crawled as her ears once more registered the presence of audio vibrations, which came from a point past the tunnel supports and with them also came a light. It was just barely visible beyond the edge of the platform.

"That better be coming from my train," Jennifer muttered, "it better not be another of those spirit trains. I don't think I can deal with anymore of them right now."

This new train came out of the tunnel. Jennifer studied it as it rolled up to the platform and her fear did not fade away until after she learned that it was solid and she observed there was a large number upon its front. It was a six. This was her train. Once it stopped and the doors open, she boarded the Number 6 train to ride it to work on 42nd Street.

# Martian Summer Dust Storm

It was the middle of the 24th century. Close to the North Pole of Mars, there existed a large city, which was constructed several centuries ago by humans and was located close to the polar ice caps. It was a night late in June. On this particular date, which put it in the middle of the Martian summer, the night was not peaceful because a very intense dust storm was attacking the city.

"No more dust," a woman's voice muttered. "Please no more dust."

Within the bedroom of the modestly seized Martian apartment, Brianna O'Casey Nunez's head tossed and turned as her very pregnant body lay under the sheets beside her beloved wife because it felt as though this horrific dust storm was very close to their door step. Her pale and creamy white skin trembled. Within her now naturally enlarged chest, the naturally weak heart of Brianna beat away in terror, she was born with a heart murmur, and tonight she was filled with a great fear not only of the storm, but also of the prospect of the dome, which enclosed the city failing to protect its citizens. Then she heard a great and horrific sound within the bedroom. After many hours of desperate but futile attempts to sleep, Brianna awoke and sat up in a cold sweat clutching the sheets to her as her body quivered in fear.

Her hijab hung around her face. "Ginny," she cried. "Virginia, wake up. Oh wake up and do so at once."

Virginia opened her eyes. "I'm up, what's wrong, Bri?" she inquired.

"That loud beeping noise," Brianna stuttered, "did you hear it? Do you know what it is?"

"Its just the standard emergency broadcast, there's nothing to worry."

Brianna made her self breathe. As she lay there, feeling her heart beat at a most rapid rate she looked beyond the foot of the bed, which enabled her to take in the very bright screen on the computer terminal, which was located adjacent to the forward bulkhead of the bedroom. Text moved across it. She forced herself to listen to the repeating disturbances. Through using the observational and the diagnostic skills she learned in her medical training, prior to going on maternity leave she was a paramedic in the city's emergency response force, she soon learned they were words.

She listened to it as Virginia sat up. "This is an emergency alert," the voice announced. "By order of the city council, a severe weather alert has been declared. A class five dust storm is currently attacking the city. This alert will remain in effect until the storm ends. All citizen are advised to seek shelter and to remain inside the city until the storm has ended."

Virginia listened to Brianna but although she did not say anything, it was clear she was in distress.

The clue was in her breathing.

It was rapid.

It was also very heavy.

Something needed to be done by someone to both reassure Brianna that she was safe and to vanish the terrible thoughts and feelings, which possessed her on this night. That duty fell to Virginia. It was very proper as she was both the more masculine one in their relationship and the more dominant one who both women saw as being the rightful and proper mistress of the apartment. Brianna was the woman of it. With her right arm, as it was the one closest to Brianna, Virginia reached over and made contact with Brianna's long shoulder length bright blonde hair and started rubbing it to put her at ease.

"Computer… computer," Brianna stammered, "Computer… Computer, end transmission of the emergency message."

The computer's voice paused before beeping again. "Unable to comply, transmission is a priority one message from the city council, it cannot be ended until either the storm ends or the message is rescinded by the city council."

"Then mute the audio."

"Order received and acknowledged."

"And computer dim the brightness on terminal."

"Working, please request reduction rate."

"50 percent."

"Working."

The audio part of the transmission ended after which the display screen lost its glow. Brianna sighed. Although the fear running through her was still present, it diminished somewhat as she felt her unborn child; she was in her second trimester, sleeping within her womb. It was a product of artificial insemination.

As Virginia massaged the petite woman's cheek, the hijabs of both women fluttered together over their blankets because they were both Muslim women, whom belonged to the reformed sect of Islam. Virginia was raised in the faith. Brianna was not as she was originally a Roman Catholic but out of love for Virginia and at her request she converted to Islam, because the woman whom Brianna desired to be with for the rest of her life made it very clear once their relationship became series that she could only marry a woman who was a Muslim. The conversion occurred two years ago. Brianna's parents understood and encouraged it, and as a sign of the gratitude, the two women regularly travelled to the largest city at the Southern pole of Mars, where Brianna's parents resided, to participate in all of the major Christian holidays. Virginia quite enjoyed them. Their marriage was one year old and they still lived on Mars, having both grown up there.

"Do you feel any better?" she questioned.

"I don't," Brianna lied. "That's not right, I do but only just a little bit.

She purred at Virginia's touch, which could almost make Brianna forget the storm was still pounding at their dome above their apartment building. Virginia starred at Brianna. "Bri," she whispered, "I can sense it's not just the emergency broadcast you're afraid of."

"You're correct, it's this storm, Ginny."

"What about it?"

"I'm terrified of it and that the dome will not make it through this blizzard intact."

At that, Virginia tilted Brianna's head up towards her own dark black face which made the bright pink silk material from which the hijab was comprised flap and the sequins decorating it jingled as the face of her blonde Irish bride was turned towards her. Brianna was the much more feminine half of the couple. Virginia starred across at her spouse and observed that her cheeks were flushed and her eyes were a dark red shade indicating she was a washed with a great state of fear.

Virginia's own hijab hovered above her side of the bed. It was plain black in color, which matched the color of her skin plus her heritage, and ancestry, which traced back to Africa. Both women were devout Muslims. Although the rules of their sect of Islam did not require them to fully cover the faces or bodies, however, over the years they were together Virginia made it understood that she preferred both of them to always still be modestly dressed and in traditional garb for Muslim women even in their privacy of their own residence. Out of love Brianna complied. In addition, Virginia decided she would always wear her hijab except when she was bathing or showering to show her devotion to her faith. Brianna followed the example.

Virginia leaned forward. She kissed the back of the hair covering the scalp of her lady who moaned. "Don't worry, Bri," Virginia said. "I'm here to protect you and our child."

"I know, Ginny, and I've always appreciated how great care you take care of me."

"Then what's so wrong?"

"I can't stop thinking about the possibility that the dome might crack or be damaged in some way."

"You've got nothing to worry about after all there are multiple layers of extra thick shielding and protection between us and the storm."

"Thank you for the reminder, but I can't stop wondering if the worse will happen."

"I'm assuming that's a dome collapse."

Brianna did not respond verbally and very meekly nodded her head. That inspired Virginia to push the side of her wife's hijab out of the way and put a small peck on the cheek in response, to which Brianna hummed. The attention from her beloved wife felt wonderful. Over the next few minutes, she both breathed and sighed, as the regular reassuring touches drove her sense of alarm away and forced her disturbing visions to retreat deep into the depths of her mind. All was well. This feeling lasted for only a few seconds before she heard another sound, which seemed to be surrounding them and coming atop of them at the same. It was the blizzard. "How long?" Brianna asked. "How long has this storm been going on?"

"If you mean just this part of it since early in the morning, which means it's been raging for eight hours now."

"I meant the entire storm."

"Just over three days."

"Three days, three days trapped in the dome."

"We're safe inside it."

"Oh, I know, but I always I see it hovering above me when I go anywhere in our section of the city. Do you know how much longer it's going to last?"

"I'm not certain but according to the latest metrology report at least two more weeks."

"This is going to be a very long storm."

Brianna shuddered. Virginia did not say anything but merely continued her most heroic efforts to dispel her lovely wife's terrors that something truly terrible would happen to their little family. The fears were understandable. In addition, although Virginia would not put it to words, she shared the great concern.

After all, the air outside their dome was extremely thin.

The ground on the red planet was covered in toxic soil and dust, which was mixed with rust.

The surface of their world was barren with the exception of the cities, the towns and the settlements, which over the last few centuries were constructed by human kind. On this world there was constant danger. It came not only from the elements but also from the constant storms which occurred but most of all from the atmosphere which included in it heavy concentrations of carbon monoxide, carbon dioxide and sulfur. There was only one defense against those hazards. That was protective enclosures to house within them the towns, cities, outposts and settlements. For Brianna and Virginia, their home was their dome, and should it crack, collapse or be ruptured the entire populace would be placed in sheer mortal peril.

For a second time Virginia kissed Brianna's head. "You have nothing to fear my dear," she stated. "It's just the storm we and our unborn child are safe."

"Virginia," Brianna whispered, "don't you think some damage might happen to it?"

"Our first child is very healthy dear."

"Not the child, the dome."

"If any damage does happen it will not endanger us as the emergency response teams are already deployed to repair any cracks and you forget about the electrostatic systems and the emergency containment systems which are built into the walls and roof of the city."

"That's true."

At that, Brianna lifted her head upwards and starred up at the ceiling. Her mind worked. On nights such as this, being held very firmly by the feminine yet strong dark black arms of the woman to whom she was the very proud and loyal wife, Virginia was an officer in the civil defense force, made her feel both at ease and filled her with a great sense of bliss.

That only dispelled parts of hear fears. After all life on their world was one of constant danger as they lived in a section of the city of Planum Boreum, the name came from the large plain upon which the city was built, and its location close to the North Pole of Mars was not an accident. It was rather a deliberate choice. Those early colonists whom came to this region of the red planet selected this area because here there were abundant natural resources in the form of heavily concentrations of ice, frozen water, methane and other frozen chemicals which could be easily obtained by drilling for them. All of these made the city self-sufficient. Manufacturing, mining and refining were three of the cities biggest industries. All of the elements taken out of the frozen plains and the products made from them were exported to other places on Mars and to other planets in the solar system. Alas, there was a trade off. Being this far North on the red planet put the citizens directly in the path of the very violent seasonal occurrences.

In winter, ice rained down on their habitat.

During the summer, it was intense storms of dust.

A hand was placed on Brianna's very plump belly. She knew it belonged to Virginia and that her skin was being massaged through the artificial silk of her bright pink nightgown. "It's good that we're both in doors Ginny," Brianna whispered. "I'd be very worried if either of us were out tonight but I'm starting to get frustrated with not being able to go outside."

"A break in the storm is predicted to occur after tomorrow night," Virginia countered. "It's going to be about two days after that before the next part of this front comes in and during that time we'll do a nice little romantic day out in the neighborhood."

"That'll be fun," Brianna cooed. "I've got a nice maternity dress that I'm certain I'll fill out quite well now and a nice pair of heels to go with it."

"I'll be starring at you all day."

"I'm glad, Ginny."

"It'll be very hard to keep my hands off you."

"That's the point of dressing up but I was thinking more of how we can't go outside the dome in these conditions and explore the plains or any of its features."

"Brianna, you're in no condition at current do any extra dome activities right now."

"Yes, dear."

"After you've given birth and once you've recovered from it, we'll go for a nice hike out on the plains together, since I at times forget my most beautiful girly girl has some tomboyish interests."

At that Brianna smiled. She opened her mouth to speak but then she heard a most alarming disturbance, which originated many miles above their very heads. She recognized it. Her hearted beat furiously in response as she felt the baby squirm within her womb because it was the wind, which was blowing the dust upon their city and it was loud enough that Brianna could hear it coming through the sides and the top of the city dome. In addition, it was very powerful and was travelling at over thirty miles an hour.

On Brianna's face, her smile faded away. As she fought to prevent tears of great distress from emerging within her eyes due to her greatly escalating sense of fright, a very familiar set of dark black fingers touch her head. They pulled on it. Brianna did not resist at all. To her great relief, Virginia brought her head down and onto her chest letting Brianna huddle there as she was petted and soft and soothing pleasantries were whispered into the ear. This felt wonderful. Of course Virginia knew what to do. She always did. Before anything else could be said, the free arm wrapped its way around Brianna's back to tightly fasten the shorter woman, without any high heels on her feet Brianna stood at less than five feet in height, into place and the fingers on the free hand were stroking the lips and cheeks of the very frightened woman.

Brianna cooed softly. It slowly turned to a little soft purr as long dark fingers went through bright blonde strands and occasionally curled them around the fingers.

"There, Bri," Virginia whispered. "There, don't worry or

panic, I'm not going any where any time soon."

"I know, Ginny," Brianna whimpered. "I don't want to feel like this, I don't want to be controlled by my dreaded thoughts."

"Then fight them."

"I don't know if I can, Ginny."

"You can Bri, I know you can because I do it every day."

"From looking at you I'd never know Ginny, you hide it very well."

"I'll take that as a compliment."

A very pleasant vibration went through Brianna. This was very delightful. As much as she wanted to relax so she could melt away into a very peaceful and very happily moaning pile of blonde Irish mush but her mind was preventing her from doing what she desired the most. It was not only the terror consuming her. At last, she understood there was raging within her a second and a third impulse which were both equally powerful but there was more for she knew that as must as she did not want to accept her nightmares did not start tonight. Brianna pondered the situation. Her upbringing in the Catholic Church and her devotion to the faith of her wife informed that she must make a confession to her most strong protector, because it was the only way in which she could finally began to conquer the frightening scenarios of her imagination.

"Ginny, it's... it's more than that," Brianna admitted, "I'm... I'm also embarrassed because of how I feel."

"Why's that my dear?"

"I've lived through plenty of storms since I was a little girl and I've been out in a few of them during training missions."

"That's true."

"I shouldn't be having these thoughts or these terrors."

"How long is that you've felt this way?"

"Since the storm began."

Virginia processed this new information. There was no need for her to wonder why this was the first time Brianna confided this to her because at once it was understood that Brianna would have thought making the Mistress of the residence emotionally care for her would be imposing an undue burden. Of course that was not so. Nevertheless, Virginia could not state that because she needed to say something that was most calming and which also contained a bit of praise.

"It's only natural that you're feeling this way, Bri."

"What're you saying?"

"You're with child now and this means that your maternal instincts, which will make you such a wonderful mother are already kicking in."

"Mmhh, well, when you put it that way I don't feel so bad."

Virgnina reviewed the situation. An idea for a possible solution, which could drive away the last embers of what was possessing Brianna occurred to Virginia and to that end she rose and slid her feet into her slippers. In just a second, Brianna's hands were grasped very firmly. That made her release a soft giggle of pleasure as she was pulled up onto her feet at a very slow rate to avoid doing any harm to the baby. Virginia let go.

"Come on, Brianna," she commanded. "Put on some shoes and follow me there's something I want you to see."

"Yes, my dear."

Virginia proceeded ahead. She walked very slowly, which ensured she would remain very close to her lady's side and detected a small set of clicks behind her, which prompted a small grin to form on her face because those meant Brianna was in her high heel slippers. Soon they arrived at their destination. That was the forward bulkhead of their bedroom. Between their respective dressers, there were a pair of large windows, which on Mars they instead called view ports as the local terminology was inherited from the initial settlers who came to Mars onboard the early colony ships from Earth. In total, there were three ports. All of them were closed tonight and were also covered with an extra thick piece of metal, which was an extra precaution taken during the long storms.

"Computer," Virginia bellowed. "Remove grates and open view ports."

"Working, working," replied the voice of the computer. Virginia put an arm around the waist of Brianna which allowed her to rest a hand on the baby pump prompting Brianna to naturally put her head on Virginia's shoulder. Their eyes watched. In front of them, all of the coverings slid up disappearing into a slot at the top of the frames and the panels over the glass, which was composed of a transparent carbon and titanium fiber mesh retracted into the bulkhead. The women stood motionless. As Virginia to Brianna's immense pleasure petted her belly, they both peered outwards to from their bedroom of the apartment, which was located on the eight floor of their building. It was located in the middle of their neighborhood, which was the old quarter.

Through the port they saw the skyline. Off very far in the distance were the four walls of the Korolev bio dome, which was a part of the city of Planum Boreum. This particular Martian city was not a traditional city. Instead, unlike the cities on Earth it was comprised of a set of domes and other enclosures, and inside of each was a large self contained borough, each of which were constructed on above basin, a mound or within an impact crater. Those all spanned the plains. All of them were connected via a set of tunnels, which held the tracks for the transit shuttles, the high-speed personnel rovers and the expressways.

"It looks very peaceful," Brianna mentioned. "And yet at the same it seems so strange since there is no one out tonight."

"They're all home with their loved ones and their family seeking shelter from this horrific dust front."

"Yes, that's true."

"Look up Bri," Virginia instructed, "and you'll see how safe we're are right now."

They did just that. High above them was the inner most level of the domed ceiling through which they saw the clouds of the leading wave of the very thing, which scared Brianna so much. All of them resembled large spirals. Many specks, of them, which were in the shape of pebbles with their unusual combination of red and orange color, came down towards the wide elevated roof.

They hit it.

Some stuck.

As she bore witness to it, Brianna felt her chest heave and a few very short breaths escaped her lips as her heart furiously pumped blood through her small body. She saw something blue travel across the translucent structure. It caused Brianna's emotional state to stabilize because she knew it was an electro static discharge and as she observed it a few pieces of dust were either dislodged or dissolved. Her heart rate decreased. She knew this enough would never accumulate to break through and threatened the life of her, her spouse or their soon to be born child.

This site inspired Brianna to not allow herself to give into her dread. Virginia pulled her eyes away to glance at the much rounder woman who stood beside her. "Do you need to see any more, Bri?" she probed.

"No, I don't," Brianna responded. "Thank you for this Ginny, this solves everything tonight. Computer, close view ports and lower grate."

"Working."

The thick material slid back into place over the ports. Then the metallic sheet came back down and afterwards Virginia removed her hand to release her wife because it was most certain she completed the task. Virginia turned heading back to their bunk. In less than a second, Brianna turned herself to follow because she knew that during this raging blizzard the one place she felt the most protected was being held in the arms of the Lady of the dwelling. Her feet moved. With each step, she felt more confident in herself and could sense the final remnants of the horrific visions that danced through her mind disappear because she at last conquered them. That is for now. Brianna was certain they would never truly vanish and knew they would always exist at the periphery of her mind waiting for the right instances and the right situations to break out and take control of her mind. She vowed to fight them so that would not happen.

At their marriage bed, the women removed their respective footwear before going back under the sheets. "Virginia, my dear," Brianna whispered. "There's one thing I want you to tell me and that's what makes you so confident the city and our dome will survive this horrific weather pattern?"

"This particular one is not as bad as the ones that our ancestors endured when the city was first founded."

"How do you know this, Ginny?"

"My great grandfather was one of the people who came to Mars during the early days of colonization."

"I know."

"He worked as one of the laborers who helped to construct this dome and the dome for the large city at the Southern pole."

"I didn't know that."

"My grandfather told me and my siblings stories about it when we were little."

With that, Virginia settled her wife's head on her shoulder and the storm raged on, and stroked Brianna's hair which made the small, devoted woman of the dwelling very happy.

"Are you over your fears?" Virginia questioned.

"I'm for now."

"That's good to hear."

"Oh but Ginny you're, right they'll always be with me now that I'm pregnant."

"What're you going to do?"

'I'll just need to fight them so that they don't control me."

"That's going to be a long fight."

"Yes, but it's one that I'm going to need to wage not only for as long as this storm exists but also every day for the rest of my life."

# Last Desperate Flight

On the rear of the starship Hayek, an interstellar cargo hauler, the large sub light engines flared as it darted rapidly through a distant star system in a most desperate attempt to escape from its massive attacker which was trailing it. Should that effort end in failure then it would mean much more than just the lost of the cargo, which was contained in its many cargo bays. It would also cost the couple that owned the small ship their very lives. The ship fired weapons. They speed towards the Hayek.

Within its small bridge, Jessica Hernandez O'Connor's eyes starred at the forward monitor and she struggled to maintain the grip of her fingers on the helm as the ship rocked around her from something which was making a hard impact on the rear electro magnetic shields. She knew the cause. It was a plasma blast, which came from the forward cannons of the Emirian raider, which was continuing to peruse the freighter even as Jessica and her husband were preparing to flee to the safety of hyperspace. The pirate ship desired to disabled the Hayek to capture its most valuable cargo.

Her husband, Kevin, starred at her. "Jessica!" he shouted,

"Jessica, give me a damage report, I need to know how badly we've been hit."

"It's coming right up," Jessica grunted. "Direct hit to our rear shields, they're holding for now at 75 percent."

"That's good to know, have we taken any damage to the sub light engines or the hyper drive?"

"Negative."

"Has the navi com finished it's work? Can we make the jump?"

"I'll need to check."

"I'm standing by."

Jessica tilted her head down. The rapid movement made her dark black hair flap over her shoulders and made her prayer veil flutter around her face as she starred at the hyper drive control panel. All of the indicators were flashing bright green. That was good. Soon they could jump. Of course that would only be possible if the navigational computer was done with its most urgent task. Under her breath, Jessica recited a short prayer to the Almighty that the calculations were already complete and when it was done, she glanced at the large navigational display, which was located in the between her and husband because that screen was in the middle of the console.

Above it was readout. Words flashed across it. Jessica read them. She swore silently to herself. Afterwards, she said a silent prayer for forgiveness after taking the Almighty's name in vain.

Her mouth opened. Before Jessica could make her report to her husband, the deck pitched sharply under her feet and Jessica was thrown rearwards into her chair as her husband fired the Hayek's reaction control thrusters and performed yet another set of evasive maneuvers to avoid being hit by the latest round of enemy fire. She groaned. Thankfully, the pain was minimized because the rear of the seat was cushioned. Kevin returned fire with their minimal armaments, which consisted of a set of low yield pulse and steady wave laser cannons, and which were normally used for destroying debris and asteroids. He looked over at her.

"Jessica," he spoke. "What can you report?"

"They scored a direct hit on us again."

"What about us?"

"We've scored a few direct hits of our own on the Emirian's shields but its not enough to disabled them or to punch through their shields to knock out their own weapons."

"About what I asked you earlier."

"Well, I've got good news and bad news, dear, because the hyper drive is fully powered up."

"I'm glad."

"But the navigation computer is still working on competing the necessary computations for us to make a successful jump into hyperspace."

"I wish our navi com was capable of working faster."

"It's an old model."

"I know."

" I keep telling you we need to upgrade."

"During out last upgrade we could only afford to upgrade the shields and the defense grid but we'll be able to upgrade it after we finish this trip."

"We need to get out of here first."

"How long until the navi com finishes?"

"Only a few seconds."

"We've got no choice then, we'll have to wait. It'll be to dangerous to try and enter hyperspace with out them."

"I understand."

That was all Jessica said to her husband. After at all, there was no point in arguing about this because Kevin and Jessica were both experienced navigators and starship pilots and they both knew how risky traveling through hyperspace was for any ship whether it was of human or alien origin. Hyperspace was a vast void. Assistance was required in order to navigate through it. Therefore, all interstellar ships regardless of whether they were military vessels or civilian passenger liners, freighters, or tankers relied upon a navigational computer or navi com to plot a course through it to their eventual destination.

There was an even greater danger. That was the task of creating a jump point so that a vessel could successfully pass between hyperspace and normal space. The calculations necessary for doing so were far more complex than any organic brain could handle. Only a navi com could perform that task.

Jessica thought. She spent much of her adult life either piloting or serving on vessels, which were ferrying passengers or freight to and from Earth's deep space colonies and its deep space outposts. From that she knew well all of the modern day ghost stories which were told by veteran space hands to first time space pilots about the danger of interstellar travel and from those she was familiar with all the horrific fates which could befall her and her husband should they attempt to make a blind hyperspace jump. That was entering hyperspace without the precise coordinates. Jessica shuddered. All that could happen ran through mind and that included the Hayek arriving at the wrong destination or becoming lost in hyperspace.

Something much worse could occur. The greatest fear off all those who travelled between the stars. Being trapped forever in hyperspace.

A terrible thought penetrated into Jessica's mind. "The Emirian vessel," she mused. "It's not going to let us go or ease up on its pursuit of us."

"It hasn't since it first opened fire upon us."

"What about its attacks?" she questioned. "What'll we do about them?"

"We'll have to buy the necessary time," Kevin answered. "I'm going to go to maximum sub light velocity."

"I understand."

"Transfer all the power you can to our shields to try and reinforce them."

"I'll do so."

"The shields need to stay up."

"I know but I'm fearful that the rear wave guides are greatly over taxed due to this little skirmish and several of the rear shield generators have already overloaded during the past bombardments."

"By pass them and tie in the secondary ones."

"I'm doing so."

"Good."

"The secondary shields are already on line."

"That should give us some extra protection."

"I hope so because the Emirian captain is not going to

stop its attempts to disable us and capture our load."

"I'm just going to have to keep going evasive."

At that, Kevin pushed the throttle forward. On the rear, the sub lights glowed. They flared. The Hayek began to greatly accelerate. In doing so it put a great strain not just upon the electro magnetic shields which protected the Hayek but also upon the structural integrity field which surrounded both the primary hull and the cargo pods and also the inertial dampers which protected the married couple from being killed by the powerful gravitational forces of their acceleration. Those were straining to compensate. Soon the Hayek was at its maximum sub light cruising speed which was just under two thirds the speed of light because no interstellar vessel went beyond that while in normal space unless absolutely necessary to avoid dealing with the time dilation caused by relativistic travel.

There was not much conversation between the couple for the next few minutes. All that Jessica said was the coordinates of enemy blasts so Kevin might try to avoid them or use their own ship based weaponry and the ship's countermeasures against them and issuing damage reports after they were hit. She tilted her head. Around her cheeks shook her prayer veil because she was a devout Christian being of the Greek orthodox faith.

Now her eyes were gazing down at the long cutaway schematic of the Hayek, which filled the center of her port console. This was the master systems display. On it she saw the entire layout of the ship and its systems within a schematic of the hull.

The Hayek consisted of a long cylindrical core. Inside it of was contained the systems as well the command and control centers and the living quarters. Attached to it were the detachable cargo pods. These were in the shape of small cylinders, which were connected to the hull by connecting struts and inside the pods were the various bays containing their source of income. That was their freight. Around the image, she saw a set of bright green lines representing the ship's shields and a set of bright green dashes, which were the secondary shields. Those helped to reinforce their meager defense screens.

As the deck rumbled, Jessica thought. Their ship was making the Hydras 4 to Altair run. The Hayek completed this particular trip many times over the last few years in which they carried ore and other materials minded in the colonies spread through out the Hydras star cluster to the large orbital space dock, which orbited Altair 4. There was also a large colony on the planet.

It was suppose be just a routine voyage. From it they would obtain the funds necessary to complete several much needed upgrades to the Hayek. Normally they spent the entire trip in hyperspace. This time it was initially true.

All of that changed when the Hayek's internal sensors alerted Kevin and Jessica, as they were on the bridge that it detected a problem, which was a weight imbalance in one of the cargo pods. In order to remedy it both of them would need to leave the core of the Hayek, and climb through the short connecting struts so they could enter the pods to determine the cause. Then they also needed to move the cargo containers around to rearrange the weight to fix the issue. That could not be done in hyperspace. As such, they were forced to return to normal space. Once the jump was plotted Jessica and Kevin found themselves exiting into this very star system from which they now trying to escape from.

Afterwards Jessica and Kevin, set the helm on autopilot, donned their respective environmental suits, and left the bridge to inspect their respect various cargo holds in each pod. Shortly afterwards the source of the problem was found. It was very quickly resolved. Alas, as they were returning to the bridge the long-range sensors alerted them to an approaching vessel, which was unidentified and whose purpose was unknown. They entered the core portion of their freighter. After removing their suits, they raced to the bridge where through a quick passive sensor sweep they succeeded in identifying it as being an Emirian pirate vessel.

Their sensors began tracking it. At once, the shields were raised. Their few defenses were activated and charged.

Immediately, they planned to jump back into hyperspace. However to their mutual anger and to their shared great misfortune before they could complete the sequence to power up the jump engines and compute an entrance into hyperspace the pirate craft advanced on them. That started their fleeing action. In response, the Emirian captain ordered a pursuit course and before the Hayek could put any distance between the two starships Jessica and Kevin found themselves being fired upon.

The console beeped. It penetrated Jessica's thoughts. She was brought back to the very depressing reality of the very grim situation that she and her beloved husband were found themselves in at this very depressive minute. She knew that sound all too well. At least she did now, because it was sounding multiple times during the many minutes know that the Hayek was dashing through this system to reach its desired safe haven and developed an unnatural dread of both it and what it meant. It was the proximately alarm. Therefore, in horror she studied the sensor readouts and as she lifted her head, within Jessica her heart sank and it was accompanied by a great sense of dread, which filled her petite body.

"We've got incoming!" she blared. "It's not a plasma blast."

"What is it?"

"This time the raider has launched a torpedo at us."

"We won't be able to out run it and we will not be able to absorb the damage. Not with the damage and the hits we've already taken," her husband replied. "How long until it makes contact with us?"

"Only a few seconds, I'm trying to get a sensor lock on so I can determine its course and its speed so we can—"

Jessica voice was interrupted. The cause was a loud ding from the navigational panel. It filled her with a sense of both great joy and as Jessica looked down at the display her, eyes lit up because he knew it could mean only one thing. She turned her head. Her bright pink lips spread open slightly revealing a very bright and glowing smile, which was surrounded by a bright pink border.

"The navi com's done," she announced. "We can finally make our jump to hyperspace."

"Good, our course is already set for Altair Station."

"I'll feel better once we're in hyperspace."

"Hold onto your seat, I'm making the jump."

With his fingers, Kevin reached over to the center of the console. He touched three large digital levers, they were pushed upwards which caused a set of massive waves to radiate outwards from all four quadrants of the Hayek's rear quarter and they all collided in front of it creating a bright circle. This was the jump point. Jessica hummed as it opened. She took in the very beautiful border, which was a mixture of bright red, green, and blue in color as the sub light engines pushed them forward. The forward quarter of the Hayek entered the jump point.

Jessica continued to monitor the sensors. From that she could tell that the torpedo was continuing to fly through space towards and would hit their stern in only a few seconds. The proximity alarm sounded. This time to her great displeasure she observed that the Emirian ship was also moving forward because it's captain she concluded must be desperate enough to make one last attempt to disable them and seize the crystalline ore, which filled their cargo bays even if that meant being caught in the backlash caused when the jump point closed. Before Jessica could warn her husband, Kevin pushed the throttle forward and in one second the entirety of the Hayek was inside hyperspace. The jump point closed behind them.

The Hayek forged ahead through hyperspace. Jessica starred out through the forward screen and she sighed because she and her husband along with their ship and cargo were at last safe.

"Next stop is Altair Station," Kevin called. "It will take us one week time to get there unless we push the engines."

"I wouldn't recommend doing so."

"Why? Did we suffer any damage to any of the engines?"

"We didn't but I'm concerned about the damage we took to the shields if we pushed the engines to much in our current condition we may have to worry about an overload."

"I understand."

"We'll need a layover there for repairs."

"How badly did we get hit?"

"We'll need to have the rear shield generators repaired along with the rear wave guidelines for the aft shields plus we lost a few power conduits and a few plasma conduits but beyond that we're still in one piece."

"That doesn't matter, as long as we're safe."

"That's true."

"Plus I've got a few surprises awaiting you when we arrived at the station."

"Oh? What are they?"

"As part of the repairs' we'll upgrade the navi com once we receive payment and the second one you'll just have to wait and see."

"I look forward to it."

# Snowy Morning Closings

Snow. It was snowing today. And it was happening here on Mars.

That was what caused Sandra O'Neil to look out through the view screens in the rear of the kitchen, which was contained within the family's habitat on Mars in amazement with her twelve year old eyes. She sipped her orange juice. Although it was for some generations now an annual event at this time of year, it still filed Sandra with a primal sense of wonder because there as a very wonderful snow coming down upon the small town on Mars, which she called home.

"James!" she called. "Do you know what the date is James?"

"I do, Sandra," James replied. "It's a Wednesday."

Her brother sat opposite her at the kitchen table. "I meant the date James, not the day of the week."

"It's December 15, 2505."

Through the corner of her eyes, Sandra observed that her brother's hands were fiddling with a small flat object but she could not identify it.

A meow was heard.

In response Sandra turned her young head. She stared at the kitchen counter and observed the families pet cat, Pike, who was running over the small-elevated platform which passed over the kitchen counter and that took him pass the other view screen that was located on the port side of the house. He stopped periodically. Sandra observed both his actions and through the transparent aluminum from which these windows shaped objects were forged she continued taking in the seemingly never ending waves of snow which descended upon their small town of Hudsonville. It was name after Captain Hudson. He commanded the first exploratory mission to Mars.

"James, you should look up from your device," she teased. "And then you'll see that it's snowing outside."

"I've seen it plenty of times before," James responded. "It's much prettier then the snow they have on Earth's but it's not natural."

"James, it's natural to our generation of Martians."

"All the snow is a product of the on going terraforming process."

At once Sandra felt her self disagree. Her younger brother, he was two years younger than her, must as her grandfather would say be daft to not be impressed with this weather pattern.

"James, where is your sense of wonder?" she asked. "Or your sense of appreciation for this?"

"I've got plenty of both, but I'm too preoccupied right now to watch."

"You should take a break to watch the snow fall."

"I'll do so when I'm done."

Sandra turned back towards the table. As she placed her glass on the table and continued with her breakfast, her eyes looked at her brother and it was then that she finally succeeded in identifying the device, which he was occupying himself with on this cold Martian morning.

"What are you doing with Dad's portable transmitter James?" she queried.

"I'm trying to get the report on the school closings that they'll be reading on the morning news broadcast."

"Where did you get it from?"

"I went into our parents bedroom and took it from our father's bedside table."

"Why did you do that?"

"I wanted to bring it down with me."

"Why?"

"So I could listen to the school closing report."

James fiddled with the controls for a while longer. He was searching through the local news stations trying to find the desired report and so he turned it into one of the local radio stations, and as Sandra finished eating her breakfast she heard something from it and so did James because he increased the transmitter's volume. His eyes lit up. "I think I've found the news bulletin!" he shouted. "I think they're going to announce if our schools are closed today because of the snow storm."

The two siblings sat there listening to the broadcast together. "The snowstorm hitting our area has delayed passenger trains," the broadcaster said. "Particularly on those rail road lines running between the city of Utopia Planitia and the city of Freeport. Caution is advised for all travelers due to the weather and delays are to be expected at all stations due to the storm."

"Did that news broadcast answer your question James?" Sandra probed

"I didn't want the report on the rail road delays," James replied. "I wanted the report on the school closings."

"That's probably coming up next."

James listened longer to the broadcast. He sighed in disappointment because the broadcaster never mentioned the school closings for Freeport County, the county on Mars in which there town was located. Thus he turned down the volume. "I need to find the news report," he muttered. "It's... it's the only way, the only way I can know if school is closed."

His palms held their father's short-range transmitter; firmly in place on the kitchen table and his fingers tapped the controls on the front of it, desperately searching for another station. "I don't think we'll have school tomorrow James," Sandra commented.

"Why's that?"

"I overheard the weather bulletin which our parents were listening to last night before I turned in."

"And what did it say?"

"Our area is going to get at least five to eight feet."

"Our schools might do an early dismal or a delayed opening."

"Most likely not."

"What do you mean?"

"It's supposed to go on through the day."

"When will it end?"

"Not until the evening."

Their conservation concluded as James focused on the task at hand. As she watched the view screens, Sandra knew well herself how the efforts of several previous generations of Martian men and women who came before her and her brother made it possible for this sight to be occurring on this vey cold morning. All Martian school children learned about it. Once many centuries ago, this was when the first colony ships landed on Mars, it was a dead world. This forced all of the original settlers to use thick enclosures to house their settlements within and in time a small thriving civilization aroused. Once those established many brave men and women ventured out to not only tamed the world of Mars but to also transform it into one on which future generations of humans could live with out these artifact habits.

To that end teams were sent up to the polar ice caps to drill for frozen water, which could be released to bringing life sustaining nature to the long dry rivers, lakes and channels which spanned the surface of the red world. And to convert the atmosphere into one, which was breathable, heroic actions were taken by miners to drill at the base of long dormant volcanoes to release ash and soot. That flew upwards into the sky. And it did not stop there but went even higher into the atmosphere and over time it mixed with the very thin layer and produced more oxygen and nitrogen. It also thickened it up. In time this process lead to the creation of Earth like seasons and weather patterns, which to the great joy of all Martian youth and their parents who were still in touch with their younger selves that also included winter.

But most of all there was snow.

On this morning it fell and blocked out her view of the residences, which lay behind and besides that of her family. And Sandra could not help but note what a sight it was as she admired it because within the long bursts descending upon the ground there was of course white but there was also bright red and bright orange.

It was truly majestic.

And it was also miraculous.

James heard a set of noises, which Sandra also registered and they quickly understood it was the presence of approaching footsteps, which were coming from the doorway. Together they looked there. The two of them saw their mother Susana Gomez O'Neil—Gomez was her maiden name—enter the kitchen in her bright green house dress and her short black heels while carrying her mug in her hands as she sipped her morning cup of tea. "Sandra," Susana scolded. "You should already be dressed for school. Go upstairs and get dressed."

"Yes, Mother," Sandra complied. "I'll do so at once."

Sandra finished her juice. She left the kitchen table and stopped at the kitchen counter to put her plate and glass in the cleaning unit, after which she exited the room. Outside the snow continued to fall. Susana and James heard the oldest child in the family go up the stairs to the second floor of the habit, where all of the bedrooms where located, as they starred at each other and now Susanna turned her attention to her youngest child.

Her voice was very stern. "James, put away your father's transmitter, we'll need to leave for school in a few minutes."

"I'm trying to find the school closing report on the news

broadcast Mother," Joseph informed her. "If school's closed today then I can go outside and play in the snow this morning."

"James, neither I nor your father were notified that your respective schools were closed today."

Sandra came back down the stairs and this time she was dressed properly for the school day. She dismounted them. It was there that she very briefly halted because through the rear screens she noticed that there was now much more than a coating of snow in the backyard because all of the grass as well as the tress and the bushes were covered by now. There was more. In addition, there were small mounds of snow back there, which despite not being very tall were still very clearly visible.

Sandra walked over to her mother. "It looks as though the snow storm is getting worse," she reported.

That alarmed Susanna. She did not show any of that to her children because she could not afford to do so. Her fingers occupied themselves in petting Pike on his chin and the back of his head but that did very little to cancel out worries about her husband. His name was Andrew. He worked in a nearby Martian town and commuted on the transit shuttles but if he did not leave the office soon he might became caught in the storm.

Susana titled her head slightly and saw how true her daughter's words were as she saw more snowfall. She was a devout Catholic. So to were her children as well as her own family and her husband's side of the clan. Susana said two silent prayers and she was asking her god to ensure that Andrew not only survived the ever intensifying storm but that he also made it home safe to her and their children.

"I've found the news report." James exclaimed. "I think

they've just gotten to the listings of school closings for Utopia County."

At that Susanna nodded to her daughter. Both of them crossed the small distance between their current position and the table and as James lifted his head slightly he saw them. This inspired him to push the device into the center. He turned the volume up so all three of them could listen to the transmission together.

"We've just received word of additional confirmations of school closings for our area," the broadcaster announced. She read off a list of towns in which all their schools were closed today because of the snowstorm. James became very excited but then the reporter suddenly stopped, which made him very concerned because the transmission was yet to mention their town of Hudsonville.

"We've just received the following additional information about the school closings for our area," the newscaster said. "All the schools in Hudsonville are closed today."

James shut down the transmitter and left the table darting pass his mother and his sister but in his haste, he left his father's portable transmitter behind him. His mother followed him. He leaped up the steps and took them two or three at a time as he went upstairs to change. Susana was concerned that he was getting ahead of himself because they were yet to received any official notification of a school closing or a snow day and so she went to the bottom of the stairwell and look up after him.

She shouted to be heard. "James, if either of your schools

is closed today then we'll get a notification from the office at your respective schools."

A while later James came back down the stairs. Now he was wearing snow pants and a shirt and in his hands he carried his black snow boots but before she could say anything, Susana heard the transmitter hanging on the kitchen wall ring. She moved over to it. Susana examined the screen on the transmitter, which displayed the logo for the Thomas Jefferson Elementary School and that was the one, which James attended.

The acceptance button was pushed down. It started to play a pre-recorded message, which lasted for a few seconds. Before she could turn to speak to her children, Susana heard the transmitter beeping again and so she once more pressed the acceptance button and this it showed the school icon for the Barry Goldwater Middle School, which was Sandra's school, but as before there was no voice playing and no vides because it was an automatic bulletin.

After this second message finished, Susana turned the transmitter off and could at last spin herself around on her high heels to see the rest of the kitchen. Both James and Sandra were standing close to her and they were starring up at their mother with both sets of eyes open wide in curiosity. It was James who spoke. "Who was it whom called?" he queried.

"It was the office at your respective schools," Susanna made reply. "Both of your schools are closed today because of the snow storm."

Susana saw the faces of her two children light up in excitement. James started off. His mother watched him going over the floor as fast as he possibly could and knew at once that he was going outside to play in the because she and her husband did the same when they were children.

"James!" she shouted. "Remember you'll need to wear your hat and gloves if you go outside."

"I'm not a tank engine pulling a passenger train mom," he jested. "That silly white stuff will not bother me."

"The cold will bother you James," Susanna scolded. "Put on your hat and mittens and don't forget to do the same thing with your coat."

"Yes, Mother," James acknowledged.

Soon he came to his destination where he halted before the long closet, which was built into the bulkhead, and was located besides the front air lock and from it he took the specified items and put them onto his body. His hand reached over. His fingers touched the controls for the port, which was constructed in a manner similar to the airlock on a starship, and started the cycle to open it. The gears hummed. By the time his jacket was zipped up the inner hatch was retracted and following a few more seconds James's hat and his gloves were secured to his body and out of the corner of his eye he could see that the outer hatch was now open.

He turned. Susanna stood there in her clothes hearing her younger child's boots hit the metallic deck plates as he rushed through it. She smiled. That was because she knew, James would soon be doing what all young people should be doing so on such a beautiful winter day and what many adults such as herself wished to do on a day such as today, which was to play in the snow.

Coming from behind her she detected the faint

impressions of more footsteps. Susanna spun around. That enabled her to watch her daughter who was dressed in her snow clothes descend while carrying her boots in her hands and she approached the position her mother currently occupied. Soon Sandra ceased her momentum. She sat down on one of the chairs to pull on her boots as she saw her mother coming over to her, which indicated she possessed instructions for her.

"Remember to only play in the yard and on the sidewalk," Susanna commanded. "And be sure you're keeping a watchful eye on your brother at all times when you're both playing outside and don't let him go into the street."

"Don't worry, Mother," Sandra countered. "I'll make sure James does not wander into any traffic."

"That's a good girl."

"Thank you, Mother."

"Now go out there and be sure to enjoy yourself."

"Yes Mother, I'll do so."

"I'll be joining you and your brother out there later."

"That'll be great fun."

Sandra rose. After donning the necessary protective garments she went through the still open front entranceway. As it closed behind her daughter, Susanna's heart warmed knowing both of her children were doing what any child regardless of if they lived on Earth or Mars should do on a snow day and that was play in the still freshly falling winter snow. And here on Mars, it was a miracle, which should be well and truly appreciated.

# Green Timbers

ain hit the sides of the green canvas tent hard. Within it a, 12-year-old year-old Boy Scout named Brian Pyle—who belonged to Troop 15 in Crab Ville, New Jersey—lay awake within his bunk because for many hours now a massive summer storm was besieging the Baden Powell Boy Scout Camp. It was located up in the Adirondack Mountains. Lighting struck something close by which made Brian's ears perk up and made his pale and creamy white Irish flesh shudder as he sat up because the noise was followed by a loud crack. At once, he scrambled out of his zero-rated sleeping bag because something very large was rapidly falling towards his sleeping quarters, which meant there was no choice but for him to leave it at once because if he did not then he would surely be killed when the impact occurred.

Brian moved fast. From underneath his cot both of his boots were procured and his feet were quickly pushed into them but they were not laced up because there was no time. This was object was fast approaching. Therefore, alas that would have to be done once he was safely outside.

His fingers went down and he took his flashlight from

inside his sleeping bag. With that done, Brain started to run towards the rear and passed the other cot, which was empty because his tent mate needed to leave camp early because of a death in the family. He paused for only a second. That was to take his poncho and his jacket from the clothing bar, which hung down from the interior of the roof of his shelter, but alas he could not spare the time to put them on. His course was resumed. Through the fabric he could sense this massive entity, which he suspected was a very tall tree, as it closed the distance.

It was almost here.

Time was running out.

He forced himself to go faster.

On the way, he started to silently pray. That was very natural because as with the rest of his family Brian was a devout Catholic and that extended back through the generations to when they still lived in the rural parts of South of Ireland. In these most desperate minutes, Brian was directing his words to his Almighty creator and asking him to ensure not only his very survival but to grant him the speed necessary to ensure that happened. He starred ahead. At once, his velocity increased and within only a few seconds, his body made contact with the unrolled green flaps of the material covering the wooden frame and he was thankful that they were not currently tied together.

He did not stop.

He pressed through them.

They parted.

Brian leapt out in the rain-soaked Adirondacks and landed on the wet grass.

As raindrops hit his shirt Brian donned his jacket and

pulled his poncho down over his body to provide himself with some cover from it. His boots were laced up. Finally, he switched on his flashlight. Then he resumed moving because he was not yet safe and through the circular shaped glow of it, he went through the night.

His boots hit the ground.

Droplets impacted on him.

Wet soil splashed on his boots.

In the distance, he could still hear the cause of his drastic flight and in process; he registered its impact on the upper most part of his minuscule bulwark. Brian did not halt. He continued his forward movement but at one point, he heard a voice speak to him within his heart and he could identify it at once because it was that of his heavenly father. It possessed one message. Now he was safe and he did not need to flee any longer, which prompted Brian to bring himself to a full stop at a spot relatively far away from where he slept for much of the night.

Coming from behind him was a great disturbance which penetrated the thickness of the deluge. Brian spun around. He starred back in the direction in which he travelled and as he suspected there was a very large log, which included branches resting on the canopy. He detected something. It was the sound of wood breaking and as he bore witness, the canopy collapsed under the massive weight and fell inwards and then downwards. Afterwards, Brian heard movement. In the distance, he spotted an individual who was making his way towards where Brian currently stood but he could not be identified through the thick downpour and so to investigate, his, his own beacon was shone into the eyes of the approaching human.

"Brian," the being grunted. "Point that light away from my eyes and do so at once."

Brian complied. His eyes inspected the individual determining that standing close to him was David Makovich. He was a tall 15-year-old teenage boy of Polish and Russian ancestry and who was the leader of Brian's patrol, which is what comprised all Boy Scout Troops.

"I'm glad you're all right, Brian."

"Thank you, David."

"Brian, what happened to your tent?"

"The trunk from the tree next to it fell on it."

"What do you think caused this?"

"The tree trunk must've snapped off from its base after it was hit by lighting. What're you doing here David?"

"I came to investigate a pair of noises which awoke me in my tent."

Brian glanced ahead. Out at the periphery of his patrol campsite, each patrol possessed their own one, he noticed a group of figures was assembling and they were peering through the dark rain-soaked area of the Adirondacks and all of their eyes were directed towards him. Therefore, he studied them. "It looks as though there are people here from all the campsites of all the other patrols and the adult leader's campsite," he confessed. "What's every one doing here, David?"

"They heard the same sounds that I did, Brian," David replied. "I think both of those noises woke up the majority of the troop and all of the adult leaders."

"Why've they come here?"

"They came out of concern, just as I did."

"Did it wake Jonathan up as well?"

"He was probably the first adult leader to leave his sleeping bag."

"I don't see him."

"He's here we just haven't spotted him yet."

It was then that a tall and rugged male figure emerged from the crowd. His name was Jonathan Powell and for many decades now he was the Scout Master of Troop 15, Crab Ville, New Jersey, and he advanced towards the scene of all the chaos. "Are you alright, Brian?" he probed.

"I'm alright, Jonathan," Brian said. "I got out of my tent just before the tree fell on it."

"I'm relived you did," Jonathan Powell replied. "What happened to your tent?"

Brian sighed. However, he knew he must repeat his earlier statement. "Lighting hit the tree next to it," Brian responded. "I jumped out before the massive log came down on top."

"David and I will need to inspect the interiors to determine how bad it is, Brian you'll need to show it to us."

"No problem, Jonathan," Brian exclaimed. "It'll take just a moment."

The three made their way to the rear of the small building. As the older two individuals looked on Brian gripped the flaps, and with a heave, he pulled them open, and with a mighty throw, he tossed them over the wooden support struts which flanked either side of the A frame. Brian moved aside. David and Jonathan inched forward and shone their small lanterns ahead of them as they peered inwards and examined the full extent of the destruction. At once, they learned that the central bar was well and truly broken because the covering was pushed down between the two beds.

Jonathan gazed down.

David did the same.

On the floor, they observed pieces of wood. Those came from the clothing bar and beside it lay strands of rope which previously held it up. There was more. Around those pieces of debris were hangs and the respective parts of Brian's Boy Scouts uniforms because those all fell when the tree trunk came down upon the structure. They were scattered around the floor. With them were other pieces of clothing such as sweatshirts and sweatpants which previously hung from the clothing bar.

"He wouldn't be able to remain here," Jonathan proclaimed. "We'll need to find a new shelter for him."

"There's an empty one in our patrol campsite," David revealed. "Brian can stay there for the rest of our time at camp."

"It's too late in the night to move all his gear David. It'll have to wait until tomorrow after we've returned from morning flags and breakfast at the mess hall."

"We'll just take what's needed for him to sleep."

"Good."

"I'll stay here and help him."

"See to it, David."

Jonathan titled his head to the side and glanced at Brian. "I'm very happily you're all right Brian. I'll see you two lads in the morning."

After saying his good byes to the two Boy Scouts, the old

scoutmaster walked away and passed the stump from which the trunk broke off.

Brian turned. He saw the group of adult leaders and scouts disperse now that their fears for the safety of occupant was addressed and their curiosity was satisfied. All of them were now returning to from whence they came but as promised, David remained behind.

"Come along, David!" he shouted. "Let's get to work."

# Derelict Ship

If one were to turn a long-range telescope on a very particular pair of star systems which is located on the periphery of the Milky Way Galaxy, and is many light years away from Earth they would be shocked to find a most strange object floating there. It is an Earth vessel. Her name is Artemis and she is a heavy cruiser. Once long ago she was a capital ship in the Terran Interstellar Navy, which since the earliest days of mankind possessing interplanetary travel has protected the citizens of Earth and its various off world colonies, but for some time now Artemis has been merely an empty hull.

However, she did not know how long, she was here because her chronometers and her time track system were severely damaged. That occurred ages ago. Back then Artemis was traveling through this particular sector space at sub light velocity because she was on a mission of deep space exploration and was mapping it when something terrible happened which was her being attacked by a vessel from the space navy of a galactic power which was hostile to Earth.

A battle raged.

Soon the enemy ship was forced to retreat.

However, the victory came at a cost because Artemis suffered extensive damage. Many of her critical systems were disabled which included her hyper drive engines and now that she could only travel in normal space, she was stranded many light years from the nearest Earth star base. After reviewing the situation her final, commanding officer, Captain Natalia Armstrong, was forced to make a most difficult decision and ordered her crew to abandon their ship in hyper drive capable shuttles in which they would travel back to Earth controlled space. The shuttles departed. Artemis's sensors tacked the small armada of refuges as they moved away from her with whatever sensors still functioned and she observed as they powered up their own jump drives and in short order all them made the jump to hyperspace. That was last Artemis ever saw of her crew.

No word was ever received from them.

Time passed.

Her crew never returned.

At some point during Artemis's new career as an empty hulk, her survival programming took over and caused her computer cores to order diagnostics run on her systems to determine the full extent of the lasting damage she suffered during that final climatic battle. The results were terrible. Her weapon systems were either damaged or could not be operated because the energy conducts which supplied power to them were disabled. It got much worse. All of her electromagnetic shields were heavily damaged, and so if she were to be attacked, she could not defend herself or fight back and with her hyper drive offline she also could not flee far. Therefore, she must hide if she wanted to survive.

This caused a conundrum for Artemis because if she wanted to be found she must remain at her current location. Her computer cores pondered the situation. At last, a solution was determined which would involve her seeking out a bolt hole which was close to her present location in which she could hide in as she waited to be retrieved by the fleet.

Not much was known about the star systems which surrounded her. And so it was that her onboard computers issued orders for a sensor sweep of each system performed so a properly informed decision could be made. Artemis waited. It took much longer than usual for the task to be completed because her arrays were only partially function which made this how ordeal a most trying and annoying one for a ship of the line but given her situation Artemis possessed no other option but to merely hang there in open space and wait. At long last, the first scan was completed.

All of the results were very informative because the system behind her contained three Earth like planets and they all orbited a binary star. Artemis knew the heat and the radiation emanating from the corona of either sun could mask her from the sensors of hostile ships if she hid there but then her processors remembered the damage to her electromagnetic shields. That would ensure the very things, she hoped to use to her advantage would instead potentially melt her hull an fry all of her circuits. That was eliminated as an option. Artemis hoped as her computer cores waited for the second scan to conclude that the other system would provide her with what she sought. The results soon came it. According to the data, the system ahead of her contained several gas giants which would provide her with an excellent cover and she also found several moons, which orbited each planet

Her processors worked.

All the information was assessed.

Then a decision was made.

Artemis would hide in the upper atmosphere of the giant which was closest to her and according to the navigational array that was the one at the far edge of the system was closest to her due to her current coordinates. A course was plotted. Her sub light fusion engines fired making so her very difficult journey began. It took a long time. Eventually, her sensors informed her that she was approaching her goal which made Artemis decelerate and another probe was conducted with her lateral sensors which determined there were no hostile ships orbiting either the gas giant or its moons. Soon she would be safe. It was then she received a most alarming report from her of her internal relays. To her shock and her dismay her fuel tanks were dangerously low because during her long and desperate journey here the Artemis used up much of the remaining hydrogen and helium 3 which were used to power both her sub light fusion engines and her hyper drive engines.

Still, she would not be deterred.

Surely all of those most important elements could be found here because the most abundant sources of them were the atmosphere of gas giants.

Her sub lights engines were switched off. Through the use of her maneuvering thrusters Artemis gently established a synchronous orbit high above the planet. She hovered there.

Another very disturbing possibility ran through her computer cores, which was that ships which belonged to an enemy power could be lying in wait below with the intention to ambush her and take her as a prize so they study her encryption codes and her technology which would greatly endanger Earth's planetary security. One last scan was performed. The results were in error because the atmosphere was interfering with her sensors and they would very likely do the same with any ship-to-ship broadcasts and therefore her main computer ordered the launching of a trio of probes into it and only a few minutes she received the telemetry.

That brought her great relief.

Contained within the atmosphere were large quantities of the much-needed fuel and there were no enemy vessels present there.

Here it was safe.

And here she could replenish her energy reserves

At last, a downward course was plotted but before there were two last tasks which needed to be performed and so she launched three sensor drones into high orbit to monitor this area of space for any star ships, which might approach her haven. With them went a pair of communications beacons. These would relay to her any hails which were received from any crafts belong to the Terran fleet.

Her thrusters fired. Artemis began her descent and was soon within the upper atmosphere of the gas giant but she knew the very strong forces of the gravitational well would surely crush her as if she were a mere tin can if she were to fall to far. That would be a disaster. To prevent it from occurring she fired her thrusters which let her maintain her position. Finally, Artemis activated her Bussard scoop. The magnetic fields stretched outwards from her position and penetrated the vast array of gashouse clouds which surrounded her and soon desperately needed hydrogen and helium 3 was moved towards her., They entered her collector. After they were processed, they went straight into her large storage tanks. As that occurred, she lay obscured within the gaseous clouds hoping that the Terran Navy would soon salvage her so she could return to active duty.

# Nighttime Patrol

## 1

It was a cold night in the middle of November. That put it several weeks before thanksgiving and the start of the winter holidays but in New York City, the calendar did not matter because the winter season was already in full swing because on this night a massive blizzard was besieging the city. Inside of the master bedroom of a small New York townhouse a woman named Jessica Flores Bey lay under the sheets in a nightgown which hid the marks on her back which were the physical indications of scoliosis, because although she did not look it, Jessica was born physically disabled. Tonight, she was wide-awake. Her eyes were staring up at the ceiling in dread and her ears were paying great attention in great terror to the non-stop and very thick noises coming through the walls and the window from the storm. Her raced. There was a three-pronged reason for this because for most of her life suffered from a very severe case of chionophopia and that was both the extreme and traumatizing fear of snowstorms. Especially bad ones such as this. From downstairs, she thought she heard something. As she considered the ramifications of it, Jessica became greatly alarmed that a human being caused it. Therefore, one phobia gave way to two more. These were the phobias of being raped and her scelerophobia and that was the dread fear of having her dwelling being broken into by a vandal or robber.

Her skin crawled. Great tears of anxiety began to form within her eyes. Before the worse could occur, her instincts seized her and at once she turned to the woman whose last name she now possessed as her own and her hand grasped the shoulder of her wife. That was Jennifer Bey. This lone act brought Jessica comfort because it was to the madam of the house that she always turned to for protection whenever she felt endangered or threatened.

The disturbance came again.

On the back of her neck, the hairs stood up.

This time it was much louder.

As such, it truly disturbed her.

## 2

As she sat there hearing the cause of her great panic, vibrate through the frame of her dwelling which Jessica wonderfully and proudly keep for Jennifer all of her light brown skin quaked in unmitigated fear. For a split second she hesitated. Then she accepted there was no other choice and she must summon her partner to her aid.

"Jennifer!" she screamed. "Jennifer, my darling I need you to wake up right now."

In a flash, Jennifer opened her eyes and sat up. Her head turned. As she starred across at the most beautiful woman that she wedded her protective instincts took over and so did those which were drilled into her by her current profession and the one before that. She leaned over. With her lips, she gave Jessica a reassuring kiss. "I'm awake, my dear maid," Jennifer said. "What has you so panicked my darling?"

"It's... it's...."

"I've long known about your fear of the winter months."

"That's what comes which being a Midwestern gal."

"If it's the storm then you don't need to worry, we're safe within the confines of our town house."

"It's not that."

"Then what has you so panic stricken?"

"I... I... I—" Jessica suddenly went silent. Her lips opened but no words came out.

Jennifer watched and started to stroke Jessica's cheeks and her hair hoping to put her lady love at ease. All of this was greatly appreciated it and for a second time Jessica tried to speak because as the gale and the frigid temperatures continued battering not only their residence but also all of New York City she knew it was of the outmost importance to inform her wife of her great concern. Her lips hung open. No words came from her mouth because as she starred over the sheets and heard the mighty wind through the walls Jessica accepted that she was frozen into being inactive. The timing was terrible. She was currently prevented from disclosing the most vital information to Jennifer and so she lay there as she received the constant and most pleasurable actions but even on her second attempt, she could not state any words.

She very tightly gripped the blankets.

No words came.

That is, until she forced herself to spit it out with her lips. "There's a," she stuttered. "There's a thing, no a person... what I mean... is I—I'm afraid there's an intruder in the house."

"I see."

"And there's more."

"Which is?"

"I'm afraid he's downstairs at this very moment."

"I understand."

"That's not the worse of it."

"Which is?"

"I'm afraid he might not just want to steal from us but that he might try to come up here and try to rape one or both of us or that he might even try to kill both of us."

"Why do you think that?"

"I hear... I hear something,"

'Which is?"

"I don't know."

"What do you know?"

"It's loud and I'm certain it's coming from downstairs."

Afterwards, Jennifer sat up. She did not doubt her spouse's words or question her concerns because the ones she raised were very valid and the last one was one that all women shared and lived with. That included Jennifer. Unlike her beloved and very petite domestic partner, she was able to better control them through her army training and her police training all of which also enabled her to create a mask of calmness upon her light brown face. It also enabled her to channel and focused her hidden fears into action. She thought. Before she undertook any action, she desired to first acquire evidence that would support the claim but only tool available to her was her ear. Therefore, she listened. Initially, the only audio detected came from the intense gusts of cold winter air which came from the storm which was raging for several hours now as it started early in the evening.

That was all.

She did a second listen.

Something was present. She was not sure what it was.

Jennifer turned. As she leaned closer to her partner, it was obvious that the shorter and much slimmer woman was on the verge of tears because a rapid pacing of a heart and a loud puffing of lungs came from Jessica and it was accompanied by a very small set of very quick sniffles. In fact, as Jennifer knew all about her wife's background and the roots of her phobia's she was now afraid than her beautiful bride would be on the verge of having a panic attack or even worse a nervous breakdown.

"Jessica my darling," she stated. "It's a cold night in November and there's a very extreme storm raging."

"I'm aware of both of those facts Jennifer."

"Why would someone want to break into our house on this night?"

"I don't know, Jen—all I know is what I detected.

"Are you confident in what you claim happened?"

"Yes... yes, I am."

"That's all I need to know."

No more was said. For the moment, Jennifer would act upon the assumption that her lovely and feminine partner was correct and would believe her instead of probing any deeper. Action was now necessary. Within Jennifer, a mental button was pressed and she went from thinking as a concerned wife to a concerned police officer. And so it was that her martial and investigative instincts which were instilled into her by her training as a military police officer during the time as an officer in the U.S. Army and as part of the training as her current profession which was as an officer in the New York Police Department took over.

"You don't need to worry any more," Jennifer announced. "I'll deal with this."

"Thank you."

Without another word, Jennifer left her place underneath the sheets, slid her feet into her slippers, and then donned her bathrobe and made her way to the small bedside table. The draw was opened and Jennifer reached into it and locked and then opened the case which was inside of it and from it she pulled out a small black revolver, which was soon loaded with several bullets which came from the small ammunition case which lay beside it and she removed a small flashlight from that same area. After a second, it was closed. Jennifer tied her robe tightly over her chest and turned to look at her wife who for emotional comfort wrapped the sheets and blankets around her very girlish figure as her eyes continued to quiver and her limps trembled.

"Stay here, Jessica," Jennifer commanded. "For the moment our bedroom is the only safe spot for you to be."

"Yes, Officer, but where are you going?"

"To investigate the downstairs," Jennifer revealed. "Close the door behind me after I leave."

"I'll do so."

"Keep the door closed while I'm gone."

"I won't open it for any reason until you knock."

"If what you fear is true this person may try to trick you, leave it closed until you hear me knock and hear me speak. Do you understand?"

"I do."

"Good."

"Again, thank you for believing me."

"It comes in the job description now I'll be back soon."

"Don't leave yet."

Jessica climbed down from the bunk. After donning her bright pink nightgown, which rubbed against her very curvy figure, she started to come towards her beloved protector and after making a brief pit stop to get something from her dresser she arrived there. She leaned in close. Jennifer examined the other woman and saw that a hand was held behind her back and there was a small but very playful and teasing glow in her eyes.

"Before you go," Jessica, announced. "I've got something for you."

Even in her high heels, Jessica still needed to stand on the tips of her toes to gaze into the face of her true protector because she was under five feet in height. That was only natural. After all, Jennifer was the one who was also the taller of the two women which was one of the things that first attracted Jessica to her because like many women she desired to be able to gaze into the optics of the person she loved. A little peck was planted on the cheek.

"Is that all?" Jennifer inquired.

"No, I've got something else."

From behind, her Jessica produced one of her black fishnet stockings. "In the days of yore in medieval England," Jessica started. "Ladies of the court would give to their husband who was their Lord or to the knight who was their champion an item of clothing as token to remind them the lady who loved them so true."

"It's much appreciated."

"It would also serve as inspiration for the knight or the king to return to them."

"And it'll do so in this current situation."

Jessica handed over the stocking before the two kissed. "Take this and come back to me soon and alive."

"I'll do both."

# 3

Jennifer came down the stairs. Her flashlight was kept close to her so it could guide her on her most urgent mission and her armament was held at her side with her fingers tightly gripping the trigger guard. All of this made her much more confident in both in her ability to complete her appointed task which was determining whether or not Jessica was right about someone having broken into their home and also about her ability to protect her most treasured partner from any evil forces which might be prowling down her on this night.

From outside she heard the continuing pelting of the walls as this massive which was expected because this cold front was expected to go through all of the night and well into the next day. Inside she sensed a rattling coming from within the walls. Both of those made Jennifer's fingers clench on her pistol. Since she was the dominant woman in this marriage, she understood exactly what was at stake tonight because no one else would be coming to her or Jessica's rescue and so she was the last line of defense against whoever or whatever perverted and devilish being maybe lurking down here. There was no other choice. Should Jennifer fail, she and then Jessica would meet a very painful, terrible and grisly death. Her fingers rubbed against the trigger because there was no other hope but her to protect the very frightened and timid damsel who was still upstairs and waited for her return.

That did not describe it fully enough.

It was more than that.

Although she was not a man, Jennifer still filled the traditional masculine role in this marriage. And as thus her most solemn duties were to provide for Jessica and to protect and defend the woman she loved and all of these strong beliefs were instilled in her by her parents. They were not the only ones. Her family for many generations going all the way back to her ancestors who originally lived in Mexico were very devout Catholics and as a child she was raised in the church. The priests of her home parish in Brooklyn drilled into her a great respect for traditional values and traditional gender roles but as much as she respected them and understood the importance of them, she was confused because she naturally identified with the masculine energy and felt better suited to the role of the man instead of femininity and the women's necessary role. In high school she at first thought that was merely because she was an athletic tomboy. During her teenage years and in she dated several men but always wondered if something was wrong with her but during her college years Jennifer, accepted she was born with a natural and sole attraction to women. Especially very feminine woman. Then everything made sense and it was her to great relief that her family and her priests were very accepting of her when she admitted the truth to her.

A squeak penetrated Jennifer's thought. As she blinked her eyes, she found that she arrived at the midpoint, of the stairway, which was, neither up nor down. Her body hesitated. Within her, there was still two voices battling and one, which told her that Jessica's alarm might be warranted after all and a smaller one which was considering that she may merely be panicking due to her irrational terrors. They were silenced by a greater force. That was Jennifer's own well-developed sense of honor and personal responsibility.

Her small but not dainty pistol was produced. She double-checked it and once its locked and loaded status was once again confirmed, Jennifer smiled because as a cop she took great pride in her thoroughness.

It was pointed forward.

Now she could properly defend herself.

With that done her downward trajectory was resumed. In the process Jennifer reflected on the experiences which her lovely other half lived before they first meet three years ago. Jessica was born in a small rural farm town in North Dakota. During her childhood, the little house wife which was how Jennifer at times refer to Jessica as, endured a very long stretch of truly awful and bitter winters in which the temperature regularly dropped below zero. It very regularly received large storms. These always left large quantities of snow on the grounds when it did not turn to ice and were always accompanied by intense and extremely chilly winds.

That was not all.

In this very frigid time of year, North Dakota would be attacked regularly by more types of frozen water, which would always fall in swift and rapid bursts and at times they would blend into each other and the storms. All of that caused Jessica to develop a very strong hatred of all weather patterns and blizzards, which occurred during the coldest, and darkest months of the year. It did more than that. Years of this impacted Jessica in a very emotional way and high school, she became determined to escape to a much warmer climate and so most of the nursing schools she applied to were located on East Coast and the one she was accepted into was in New York City. Upon arriving she fell in love with it. Within a few months of her first academic term, she was very glad to have a much milder winter but there was a danger she experienced because the only room she could afford to rent was on the border of a very bad neighborhood because it and the ones around it were very economically depressed areas. There crime was rampant. During the four years of nursing school, she lived with a daily fright of her room being broken into whether or not she was in it and of being assaulted and having very horrible acts done to her even when she was not out on the street. All of that scared her. Her years living there were also left a great but terrible impression on her and was responsible for her developing her second irrational fear, which was her fear of being raped and her third and that was of her sleeping quarters being, stolen from.

It did much more than that. All of this created within Jessica a desire and a need to help those who were less fortunate than her and who her victims of criminal actions with her medical skills and especially women. Soon she graduated. After a few rounds of applications and interviews, Jessica was approached by private practices, clinics and medical research facilities to come work for them but Jessica turned them because she wanted to work in a public role. The state health department approach her but being a lesbian woman Jessica possessed a strong distrust of government. To support herself she worked as a maid in hotel. There she refined her very masterful housekeeping skills and after a year doing this she was hired as a trauma nurse in one of the New York public hospitals.

That led to how the two women meet. This was back when Jennifer was still a patrol officer and spent her shifts driving around in a patrol car. On that most wonderful night, Jennifer visited the hospital on police business, which involved her bringing a person who survived an armed robbery of his store there to be treated at the hospital because he took a bullet in his shoulder. Jessica was the admittance nurse.

Soon afterwards, they began to date. The two gals

bonded over their shared background of being Hispanic women even though there were some cultural differences between them because Jennifer was born and raised in the city instead of a small town and was also raised in the Northeast instead of any of the Midwestern states. That was not all. Both of them soon they discovered they were both raised in a moderately conservative Catholic family whom balanced out both their conservative and libertarian beliefs. In addition, both of them were only romantically interested in women. This was something which Jessica discovered in her first year of her medical training and at first, it confused her but after a while, it made sense to her because out her closest circle of friends in high school she was the one who was the least interested in men. Furthermore, both were devout Catholics. Although they did not agree with the Catholic Church's stance on gay or lesbian marriage, they did agree with it on other teachings and supported the core message of the church and its core values.

One year later, they moved into together. Then they lived in a small apartment which Jessica kept neat and clean when she was not working. Only a few months later Jennifer was promoted from being a patrol officer to being a plain-clothes officer and was reassigned to the New York City Police Department's Anti-Crime Unit. Following, her transfer Jennifer asked Jessica for her hand in marriage. Without needing to think at all, Jessica said yes and happily let her dominant partner put the ring on her finger.

They were wedded in the back yard of Jessica's ancestral farm house. On that day Jessica became Mrs. Bey or as she loved be called just Mrs. Jennifer Bey because as the two of them were both traditionally minded woman despite being lesbians they desired to show everyone else which of them was the wife. Following their wedding, they moved into a nice neighborhood in the borough of Queens, New York. That was where they currently lived. The best part of it was they did not need to buy it or take out a mortgage from a bank to get it or make a down payment on it. Instead, it was a gift. It was given to them by Jessica's grandfather who among his other business ventures ran a very successful real estate company and owned property in the city. This was his wedding present to them.

# 5

For a third time, Jennifer over heard a large rustling. It prompted her recall to conclude and now she learned she was standing on the last rung of the steps, her lips furrowed, and her eyes tightened because now she was solely focused upon her mission. It was time to conduct her first visual sweep. She pushed her beacon forward and moved it across all of the wooden planks as she scanned it with her own small visual telescopes.

None of the lights was activated.

At least none that Jennifer could see.

That was good.

It brought a relief to her because it indicated there was no intruder in here.

She came onto the floor. As Jennifer terminated her movement another scan was performed but it led to the same results. Within her brain, her next course of action was debated because she desired to go back to her mattress both out of a strong craving to be once more under the warm covers and a strong desire to check on Jessica was now surely at her most vulnerable and desperate because she was surely within in a very terrifying state which was created by all of her phobias and reporting her findings would give to Jennifer the chance to check up on her. Her guardian nature seized control of her. She was not yet convinced that there was no vandal down because he might be elsewhere, he could not yet be found and therefore, she would need to remain here and take the necessary steps to ensure the safety of her household.

Once more her police training took over. This told her there was only one way to ensure the safety of both herself and her beloved wife and that was to search the entire floor. On this level, there were four rooms. Before she could be convinced it was well and truly safe, she needed to enter each one. clear it and it needed to be done in a sequence pattern which would take her eventually to the back door. This meant she must start with the family room. That was the closest one to where she stood. Beforehand, she would need to undertake some necessary perquisites and so her light stick was switched off because it might give away her position. Her armament was raised. Then she moved out relying upon her own knowledge of the floor.

To her great confusion, she could have sworn her audio sensors were registering the presence of a very soft but still present disturbance. She briefly halted. Out of a great fright, that the person she was here to find might be aware of her and was approaching her from the other direction Jennifer made herself halt. Her fingers switched off the safety on her pistol because she might need to confront him fast and would be required to fire in a microsecond.

The audio penetrations came again.

Jennifer froze.

She paid closer attention and determined it was coming from all around her which puzzled her but she decided that there was no need for her to remain here. Jennifer lifted her slippers. With her pistol, pointed ahead she resumed her patrol but decided to not switch the safety back into place because there would be no point because if she were to come, across this hypothetical intruder, she would have to fire at once and there would not be time to waste releasing it.

Ahead she went. In under a minute, Jennifer entered the living room. There she halted so she could examine the area, which lay immediately ahead of with her dark brown eyes. There was no one there. All that could be found was a couple of couches which were spread out and around which were a set very comfortable lounge chairs that were arranged in a circle.

These were also a gift. They were given to Jennifer and Jessica by Jessica's parents who invested very well in technology startups and all of the furniture was both a wedding present and a house warming present. For a third, time the vibrations came. Now Jennifer's eyes darted around because their queries and ponderings forming with her mind because they were coming from all around her and so he focused on them and determined it was a creak. They came from beneath her. On her first audio inspection, she thought that it was only one source. After a closer listening, she learned it was also behind her and in front of her at the same time which she thought now maybe movement of the adult male Jessica thought she detected. Further attention was paid. It was not a human which created them because all the sensations were being produced by the floorboards and the pipes but there was still no one in here except her lonesome and confused self. Still Jennifer continued onwards.

# 6

The next place to inspect was the living room. A quick and detailed probe of it was conducted but she again found nothing here that was moving well other than her that was. She lowered her pistol. It took a few seconds to reorient herself and then she went towards the dining room which was the second to last compartment on this lower half of the facility and very swiftly she came into it and on this cold and very snowy night, which fell early in the winter, she found only furniture in it. Her mission was almost complete. There was one last room for her to subject to her scrutiny, which was the kitchen, and once it was clear then at last Jennifer could head back up to her spouse. So, she headed towards it.

A few seconds passed. Once she stood between the sides of the hatch, Jennifer temporally paused in her forward movement, because although she was almost done, she was very worried about the possibility that she was becoming overconfident in herself. That would be a fatal mistake. Especially, if there were a violent and evil man who was lurking within the final chamber and who was armed with a weapon which would mean it would be her undoing.

Jennifer peered in front. No one was found inside of it and so she inched forward at a very slow pace and on the other side she froze because she was conducting a second visible inspection of the area but that only produced the same results. She kept her fire arm still. There was a very slim possibility that the still present darkness was interfering or obscuring with her visual noticing of activities in this rear most portion. Light was needed. Her fingers slowly moved over to the light switch and flicked it upwards which brought illumination to the area and provide to Jennifer, the final proof that only her and her surely anxious spouse were the only ones in the entire building.

"I'm done," she noted. "Jessica was wrong and I'm happy for that but now I've got to go and tend to her."

She lowered her service revolver. The safety was pulled back into place and she wondered what her beloved Jessica could have possibly heard that would make her suspect unusual activity down here in the first place. The exterior. Jessica must have overhead heard something or some other vehicle on the street and, all of her phobia translated that into what she feared the most, and so after a few seconds, Jennifer came to the back door. She peered out through the glass. All that could be spied in the backyard was snow covered grass but for the sake of being through she switched on the rear outside lights, which provided her with a clearer view, but it was the same. In short, order they were deactivated.

Jennifer turned around. There was one last place to check, which was the front of their residence, and within a few minutes she was at the front door and repeated the same procured. Nothing could be found. Now that her task was well and truly done Jennifer turned and started heading back to bed and to the woman, she cherished so true and who was surely in great need of her care.

# 7

Upstairs in the bedroom a different scene was unfolding. As soon as Jennifer departed, Jessica Flores Bey found she could not resume her so greatly craved rest and could not remain under the sheets because they reminded her of how the other half of their marriage was putting themselves in danger because of her

Therefore she found herself here. Jessica's body was pointed dead ahead and out of great anxiety her eyes were locked upon the interior of the sole hatchway and she was currently only a few inches away from it. At current, it was closed. That was because Jessica obeyed her wife's instructions to the letter after she departed upon her late-night quest.

Her hands clenched. As she waited for the lady of the house to return to her, her lips were quaking, and every inch of her skin felt as if it were trembling because she was on the verge of panicking and releasing large wet and diamonds shaped objects from her tear ducts. Something rubbed against her. Her eyelids fluttered rapidly.

"Oh, no!" she screamed. "Please get it off. Oh, Jennifer, help! Jennifer, come at once, oh Jennifer, where are you?"

Her fingers flexed open and closed several times. "Calm yourself Jess," she muttered. "It's just your hair and your own clothes but your woman will be back soon and then very thing will be all right. There's nothing to fear. Not at all, not when Jennifer's out there."

She adjusted the side of her robe. Although she wanted desperately to believed herself Jessica knew only too well that she was lying to herself because she became so deeply disturbed over the long but surprising limited minutes that she was here. Her grip on the fabric tightened. As she rubbed it, she understood the reason she pulled on this robe was because it was engagement gift from Jennifer, which made her understand she was on some level trying to counter and contain her phobias by cradling herself in a repression of Jennifer's protection.

More bits of winter hit the window glass.

Then it attacked the sides and the roof above her.

Jessica almost jumped.

On the outside, she was calm and collected. As much as she missed Jennifer, she was very glad she was not here because this was a mere act which was rapidly falling apart and what was more, she would not feel right at all while Jennifer was still downstairs. Fluffy white flakes impacted on the window glass. Jessica blinked her eyes and knew as she struggled to prevent herself from screaming and tapped her slippers on the ground, she knew the culprits lay within her which were her phobias, which were responsible because all of them, being raped, having the house broken in and the storm were all against her well-being and her sanity. They united. Now they were acting as one massive force which was armed to the teeth to conduct psychological warfare against her by continuing to unsettle her in Jennifer's absence from her side.

Her now very alert early warning systems detected something which came over the exterior effects of the winter blizzard and as she paid closer attention to them, she soon understood that was she was wrong. It was a group of vibrations. They came from the interior. Correction they were in the hallway and they were moving along it which meant they were moving towards her current shelter and would be here soon.

Her heart felt as if it stopped. Jessica struggled against

allowing her great terror from making her unable to think at all because they were increasing in both volume and their clarity, which meant they were also getting ever nearer to her. Now she was terrified. This functioned at a level beyond a mere concern for her mortal form because Jessica possessed no knowledge what so ever of what happened to Jennifer and was worried that his intruder harmed her wife or worse killed her wife.

Her lips trembled. As she advanced from the bed towards the door in a morbid combination of curiosity and great fear Jessica forced her to not panic. Her eyes went straight ahead. For a third time it came through the walls and now it was at its loudest and at her sides Jessica's fingers were pressed into her palms because they were now very close to the sole barrier which existed between them and her.

# 8

She forced herself to breathe. Between each rapid and very brief inhale and exhale, Jessica considered her situation and noted she was alone, without her normal defender. In addition, she was defenseless.

The source of these strange footsteps approached the hatch. Jessica forced herself to remove her eyes from it and she glanced around the sleeping quarters be she knew that in a very short time she would be forced to fight a life-or-death battle. That would be most difficult. When she departed earlier, Jennifer took with her what was the only gun not just in their sleeping quarters but also in the entire abode, which left her with nothing to protect herself with. Jessica fretted. Once again, she questioned whether or not Jennifer was still alive at all and also if she encountered the walking object which was the cause of her great terror and if so if she survived the experience. Her skin shuddered. The prospect that Jennifer failed or was dead needed to be forced out of Jessica's mind because any moment now she would be within a life-or-death struggle in which she would have only one chance to preserve herself from certain death. Her thoughts need to be in here and now.

"If Jennifer were here, she wouldn't just lay down," Jessica mused. "She wouldn't let herself become parlayed, and she wouldn't give up, she would stand her ground and fight."

That made Jessica realized there was only one option. She must fight this battle on her own but that would require her to have something to use to fight off the presumably hostile force and so her current situation made her wonder what her partner would do. The solution occurred that she must make an improvised one. With that Jessica pivoted. She went across the bedroom and came to her closet where she parted the dividing doors and then leaned down looking into the very bottom of the closet, and grasped two objects. She stood up. In each of her hand was a pair of high heel shoes.

"Yes," she stated. "These will do nicely and after all these are the best and only thing I've got to work with."

She examined her choices, which were dark red. They ended in a very large point and underneath them were four inches of heels and the points of them were both very long and sharp. Jessica grimaced because she was trying to force all of her fears which were still very much present within her so that she could accomplish this action of last resort. She fretted. This was not her natural environment. Acting on her own was something she often felt very uncomfortable doing when it was not something that was part of her nursing profession or the domestic work and house work. She briefly wondered if her madam failed or not. That was buried very shortly because the steady clicks on the ground were now almost at the entrance to what was supposed to be her own sanctum.

Jessica moved fast. In a short period, she was standing just on the inside of the gateway and raised the footwear above her head so that she could act in her own defense. These very blunt and point instruments would be very useful against anyone who came through the last barrier between them and her and especially if that was the violent criminal of whom she was so petrified of doing terrible things to her.

She heard a knock on it, which came from the other side.

It was followed by a woman's voice.

At once, she knew her protector returned. "Open the door, it's me, my darling wife."

# 9

Jessica dropped her weapons on the floor and her still shaking fingers grasped the handle, and at the slowest pace possible, she turned it and the hatch was opened. She purred. A big smile appeared between her lips as she moved in reverse by just a section of an inch and allowed her returning valiant and alluring protector to enter their dormitory.

"Oh," she exclaimed, "I'm so glad you're all right. Did you drive away the intruder?"

"There was no intruder downstairs my sweet."

"I'm sure I heard something Jennifer."

"You must've heard the pipes."

"Perhaps you're right, I'm just glad there was no one there."

"So am I."

Following that Jennifer came inwards. At the sheer sight of the Madam of their household, Jessica felt herself becoming over whelmed with joy and so she jumped up into the air and forward by only a few inches to give her a big hug. It lasted for just as second. Then Jessica retracted and she picked up the high heels and pretty much skipped in her bare feet as she took them to the still open clothing unit to return them. That task took less than a second but she was annoyed when she stood up, she was annoyed to learn Jennifer did not follow her as she desired but was instead going to stow her armament. On the surface level, Jessica understood that. On a much deeper level she was annoyed. Although the threat was gone, Jessica was greatly craving the embrace that could only be provided by her spouse's arms and the warm feelings of being safe and secure within them because she was still recovering from the long and extended period of terror, which plagued her so deeply and now it was also mixed with a tinge of regret for being responsible for having sent Jennifer on a massive wild goose hunt.

At the mattress, Jennifer halted. Her fingers pulled open the fire arm and the ammunition were removed so it and the light could be properly stowed in the table. The draw was closed. With that one final thing completed, Jennifer turned and from merely glancing at Jessica's cheek from this angle she could infer that she was still worried or rather, she was now embarrassed about the way she behaved and that meant her work was not yet done. The woman she loved must be reassured. And so at once Jennifer started over the wooden surface to the woman to whom she pledged herself to for the reminder of their mortal life and soon Jennifer crossed to the closet where she spun Jessica around, took her by the hand, and pulled her in close for an embrace which made Jessica giggled softly in excitement.

Jennifer stroked and then kissed her lady wife's cheeks.

"We're both safe my darling," she stated. "There's no one here that can threaten the lives or the liberties of either of us Jennifer." She kissed her wife's lips. "Your fears were well founded given your past experiences and you possessed every right to feel that way."

"Thank you, Jen, thank you."

"You're most welcome."

"And thank you for taking my claims so seriously."

"It comes with the job."

With that Jennifer pushed the head of her beloved matrimonial help mate down onto her shoulder and ran her fingers through the strands. Jessica hummed. Now she was feeling much better about having been afraid earlier and having given into her trio of great terrors because she thought for even a mere fraction of a second that she heard movement within their sanctum earlier.

"You're right my dear," Jessica purred. "There's nothing for me to fear. Not when you're here, Jennifer, to protect me and keep me safe."

# Nighttime Rail Liner

It was a winter night in the year 2461. At that precise moment I was heading home from seeing an evening showing of a recently released movie in the nearby commercial district of my neighbor which was located only a blocks distance from my residence. Instead of driving I walked. My decision was inspired by the wonderful weather which was provided by the environmental control office of the massive domed city which I called home. Given the latest of the hour I decided to take a short home. That involved me taking me a quick detour to the local rail station and going down the steps to pass through the tunnel which ran underneath it and as I came up the steps on the other side of the station where I heard a great nose. It startled me for it indicated a large object was rapidly coming towards me.

At once I moved over by just a few inches. Behind me was the large public park and on the side of it was my home and beside me was the station house but it closed to the public hours ago. The sound came again. In response, I decided to investigate which led to my head spinning around and my artificial eyes, which were surgically implanted in me as a child because I was born blind, starred down the rails and saw a square metallic shape racing towards me. Surrounding it was three large lights which glowed through the air of the domed city. The shape was recognized at once. It was an engine which was pulling a regional shuttle towards me and it was coming from the next stop over on the magnetic levitation tracks and at once I was able to identify the still lingering audio productions.

First there was a horn.

It was blowing and afterwards a brass bell rang.

Then the horn sounded again.

Other than myself there was no else here at the station but still this was a standard signal which was issued to alert anyone who was waiting for the train to arrive that it would be there soon because the driver, the person who guided it, and the conductors who worked onboard possessed no knowledge as they made their way up and down the line of it there was nay there waiting for them.

It was starting to come close to my position. This allowed me to see the whole extent of the locomotive which was tall and silver in color and in the middle of the side was a stretch of multi colored paint. Behind it were five cars. They were all coupled to the machine which pulled them. Still, they were too far away from me to see through any of the windows which were located in the side of the frame but surely as it neared this part of the city some of the travelers would be packing up all of their belongings and would be starting to move along the aisle which divided the seats into two separate columns. Their destination would be the car doors. Since I travelled on this line during the week to commute to and from work, I knew the hatchways were located in the front and rear of the carriages.

As the commuter rail cars drew ever nearer to where I balanced on the paved sidewalk a faint spark was noticed which was just out of range of my vison. My brain worked. Commands were issued which directed both my scanners down towards the bright gray rails and saw underneath the locomotive and its charges and coming from there was an electromagnetic current. The color was blue.

All of this caused me to recall the lessons taught to myself and my sibling in grade school about the manner in which this system operated. It started with the generator which was located underneath the bottom of this massive machine which was pulling the rest of the commuter train and which sent an electrical current was sent down through a series of wave guides to each round object. In the center was a large magnet. Those were in turned surrounded by a set of metallic wires which created a circular encasing and as the motion occurred within each one it in turn created the electromagnetic field necessary for the regional shuttle to cruise at a velocity of many miles per minute. Each carriage was outfitted in this manner. Within the forward most portion of the electrically powered engine there was a small cabin containing a large console which allowed the driver to control the functions for every device.

Forward it went. Based on its position I was able to deduce it was on the outbound tracks and so would be coming into this particular stop across from where I was standing. Given its current rate of movement I estimated it would arrive in under a minute and sure enough after that thought raced through my mental processors, I realized the force running under the respective parts of the transit line was diminishing because it slowed and now it was coming up to the platform. All of the cars bounced on their spinning generators as the driver brought his command to a full stop and applied the brakes which ensured they remained motionless. Time passed. No more of what was occurring could be seen my small visual telescopes because the hatches which would be opening now to let those for whom this was their stop leave was beyond my line of sight and for a few minutes this collection of machines which was used by commuter line sat there.

Then the electrical motor started. An electromagnetic current ran underneath the engine allowing it to accelerate along the magnetic levitation tracks and under the passenger cars, an electromagnetic current passed through the wires providing them with propulsion as they followed the engine. Forward the shuttle started. Immediately as the wheels started to rotate the elector magnetic energy was generated and allowed all parts of the commuter line to accelerate down the line to the next station and as all of the induvial components clanked on the tracks the headlamps shone ahead to guide the way. The familiar audio productions from earlier occurred again. Soon the next bend was reached and this late time transit liner went around it and within a few seconds it disappeared into the winter sky and shortly afterwards all of the vibrations dissolved into nothingness.

No longer was there a reason to remain here. And so, my feet turned me around and my homeward course was resumed. Within in a brief span of time, I was walking up the steps to the front door of my dwelling when my visual scanners chanced to observe the relatively round silhouettes which were shinning down on me from above through the translucent dome prompting me to look up as they came into view. Without a second's hesitation they were identified.

The two moons. Of the world I called home for the better part of my life.

The inner one was named Phobos. It was also the larger one. As for the outer and small one it was called Deimos.

On this very night they were orbiting very close to the planet of Mars on which I lived for my entire adult life and before I went through the front hatch, I thought briefly about how the cites upon the moons were visible tonight.

# Demise at Midnight

Tomorrow morning would be a momentous occasion. At least it would be for, Patrick Stevens if his beloved wife Marianna was still alive, because tomorrow was their 50th wedding anniversary but instead of celebrating he was filled with dread because he felt a strange presence surrounding him in his room within the retirement center on the Jovian moon of Io. He clenched his hands. After a quick scan of the room, he saw only himself but still he felt the essence draw closer to him and so needing a distraction he turned his head to star at the photos on the bedside table. Behind them was the time piece. To his horror the digital readout ominously flashed 8:00 which caused him to fear his death was imminent.

"Oh no," he groaned. "Oh no, not on this night, please Lord don't let me die now."

He was worried because his heart was weak both as a product of his age which was eight, his heart being weak because he was born in the weak gravity of Io and spent his life there and also because his body was still recovering from a severe chest cold. His ears twitched. At once Patrick craned his neck forward because he was certain he overhead a feminine voice speak to him but although he was certain it was familiar he could not identify it and to his confusion it was calling its name. A bright light appeared. Seeking to dispel his fright Patrick sought comfort in the wedding photos but he came to regret that because they were all covered in a bright light. His attention turned to the one in the center. It was the tallest and it was also his favorite because it showed him in his suit and Marianne in her wedding dress but before his eyes the frame shimmer and that spread inwards to the picture.

"I never understand," he muttered, "I never understood why she wanted to fold the veil back over her face for the photo when it was taken after the ceremony concluded."

"Because my dear," someone stated, "I was so happy I was afraid the glow in my eyes would ruin the picture."

Patrick recognized the voice at one. He redirected his gaze and his eyes went wide in amazement because he saw Marianna or rather her ghost floating just beyond the edge of the bed. Within his veins, Patrick felt his blood race in a mixture of fight and passion because all of his feelings for her which never went away after her funeral came to the fore and as he studied the translucent form, he learned the representation of her spirit was free of any evidence of the damage wrought to her body by the disease which claimed her life after a long battle. That happened years ago. Something trailed underneath her and following a closer inspection he saw she was clad in a glowing recreation of the red dress and the matching high heels which she was buried in.

Despite all of this Patick was still confusion. "Marianna?" he asked. "Is that you?"

"Yes, my dear."

"Where did you come from?"

"Heaven of course."

"What are you doing here?"

"My handsome husband, I'm here to see you."

Patrick thought. Over the years since her demise, he felt Marianna's presence around him and he also at times swore he heard her voice speak to him but he was never able to see her spectral being until now. Given his still weaken physical condition, he felt short of breath because. Although he was happy to be reunited with the woman he loved and who bore him several strong sons and beautiful daughters he was seized by terror because underneath these feelings was a well-formed sense of dread that her appearance here on this night foretold his demise. Marianna watched him. As his ghostly lover floated around the side of the bed and approached him, Patrick sensed a tightness form within his chest but he was distracted from that when noticed how the wonderful reaction of her silverish white hair was not floating at her side as it when she was buried but was instead tied up in a top knot. That was how she wore in the final years of her life.

"Why?"

"Because I love you."

"Why tonight?"

"Because of our special day, the Lord of the universe allowed for my soul to spirit to return and because of what is to come soon."

"Our anniversary is tomorrow."

"I'm afraid your time piece is broken, dear."

"What do you mean?"

"It's already midnight."

"That means, that means..."

His voice trailed off. "Yes dear, fifty years ago today I gave myself to you as your bride and in the eyes of the law and the Almighty I became Mrs. Stevens."

"Then there is nothing to regret."

"What do you mean?"

"I can die happily since I made it through to that day."

Marianna's form flickered. This caused her outfit to be replaced by her white wedding dress which was completed with a long trail going down her back and a pair of see through gloves which enclosed the upper half of her arms. His vision went to her face. It was covered by a white but shimmering veil and she brought her arms up and somehow, she managed to grip the edges and folded it back exposing her face and then Patrick saw the previous color was replaced with a goldish shade of bright blonde which was her natural hair color. Or it was until she became old. Out of the corner of his eye, Patrick noticed the central photo glow bright and he watched the picture of him and Marianna suddenly alter itself because it showed them being much older and then reverted before showing them as children. That did not make sense. The two of them married when they were both in their mid-twenties.

"You still have all the photos of that day," Marianna commented.

"I could never get rid of them."

"That was a wonderful day."

"Yes, it was."

"Our whole future lay ahead of us."

"Back then we were full of youth, vigor and optimism."

"And I was thinner and more beautiful then."

"You never stopped being lovely in my eyes."

"That's sweet."

"And I always thought you became prettier with each subsequent pregnancy."

"Why is that?"

"Every time you became pregnant you also became curvier."

"You were always a charmer." Marianna leaned down. "How long has it been?"

"Fifty years."

"No, since I left you."

"Fifteen years."

Marinna gave her husband a kiss and to Patrick's alarm his face did not pass through her face but instead made contact with them because in this moment his beloved lady's lips were solid. Marianna pulled her face back. From within his form, Patrick could feel the dangerous rapid pounding of his heart and the heavy beating of his lungs but now he was now longer scared instead if anything, he was happy because those previous feelings gave way to a sense of relief. That was soon replaced with a tranquil bliss. Then he saw that his surroundings and all of the furniture were a washed in a bright gold light.

"What—" he stammered, "what's happening?"

"Explanations aren't important right now," Marianne answered. "Those can wait."

"But I want to know."

"You've lived many long and hard years since I was taken from you husband."

"I missed you every day."

"So did I but now it's time for us to depart."

"I don't understand."

"You'll do so in time as I did."

"Yes, dear."

"Where are we going?"

"On a journey."

"What's our destination?"

"I'm confused, I'm home."

"I'm not referring to this place husband but to the home from which your eternal soul came from."

Marianna placed finger on her still living husband's lips. "Now put your head back down upon the pillow," she instructed.

"Yes, dear."

Patrick did as she commanded. To his shock Marianna lay down beside him but although her presence was reassuring, he was terrified that he could feel her wedding dress rub against his clothes and hear her earrings shake and her veil flutter because now all of her attire seemed to have some faint physical presence. Before he could give it any further thought, Patrick experienced a sharp pain which came from within his shoulder and he was certain his death was close at hand and as such his upbringing in the Catholic Church seized control of him.

"If I die," he muttered, "If I die…"

His voice trailed off because it was becoming hard for him to breathe but Marianna concluded the prayer. "I pray the Lord my soul to take."

"Yes, dear."

Marianne reached over with her fingers and Patrick was shocked she was able to clasp his with it. Once more he gazed at her. While he admired her, he discovered her appearance went through an amazing transformation and now she was 27 which was the specific age she was when they married and as he she also altered the way in which her was styled so that the held up in a high resting ponytail. That was how she wore it when he was courting her.

Although he could still produce words with his mouth, this time it was difficult for him to do because his voice was raspier than before.

"So," he muttered, "so beautiful, you're still so beautiful after all these years."

"Thank you, dear," Marianne made reply. "And you're still very charming."

She kissed his cheek. While they remained there on the

bed, Patrick felt a sharp pain but this time it was not only occurring within his shoulder but also in his chest and as large puddles of sweet fell down his brow he struggled to inhale and then a massive explosion occurred inside of his torso which resulted in his heart stopping and his pulse expired and his lungs ceased any action.

His eyes closed. His hand came lose. It fell down on the bedsheet.

Patrick was dead.

Marriana caused herself to smile because soon they would be together. A portion of her light from her and travelled across the bed to Patrick whose form it soon enclosed which inspired her to command herself to rise because his skin and clothes were the same color as her. Having died she knew this energy field came from the ruling monarch of the next realm to which they now belonged and she dared not interfere with this process because he was more powerful than any spirit or any mortal science and he was also older than humanity and the universe. Another soul would be arriving soon.

From the ceiling, beams emerged. They went down hitting Patrick and moved over him as if they were scanning him and then they shot out towards Mariana.

She moved over to her right a few inches.

All of these beams concentered in the air and after a flickering of the light the ghostly outline of Patrick's essence emerged and he starred at his wife and then back at the bed before he spoke. "What happened?" he asked. "What happened to my body?"

"You're dead, dear," Marriana answered. "And now we're together again."

"Why is my body lying there?"

"You no longer need it."

"What do you mean?"

"Your spirit has been freed from its physical shell so that it can move onto the next phrase of your existence."

She wrapped her arm around him. This time her image flickered and did so along with Patrick's and following a second Marriana was once again clad in in a recreation of her wedding dress and Patrick was now wearing his suit from the day, they became bound in blissful matrimony. Together they floated over the floor. As Marianna wrapped her arm around her man's a unique energy flowed through them. It was a metaphysical representation of their bond as man and wife which was created on the day they were wed and through the years they were married it was strengthen many times because of the trials, the struggles and the tribulations of their life together and what they endured. Behind them a bright blue door appeared. Marriana caused her husband to turn around with her and if he still possessed a physical body, it would have fallen open and his eyes would have gone wide as he took in the sight.

"Come on, dear," Marriana stated. "It's time to go."

"Go where?"

"Why to the place from which all souls come from and to which they all return at the end of their life in the realm of mortals."

Off they went through the door which closed behind them and shimmered before vanishing. In its place all that was left was a now useless physical shell which the attendants would find in the morning as they performed their routine bed check.

# Corpse on the Tombstone

The sand was everywhere. Alas, Marla Chen was unable to appreciate its beauty for it was being blown into her face and was thrown against her body by the wind from the dust storm which was attacking the marble walls and columns which enclosed this area on Mars because as she knelt in an ancient cemetery which predated the existence of humanity her mind was on more pressing business because in her arms she cradled the immobile body of her husband. His name was Dominic Watson. Something terrible happened to him minutes ago after he encountered a horrible grave and so between her non-stop sobs, Marla was issuing an urgent distress call.

"Help!" she screamed. "Please somebody, anybody help me. It's my husband, he's been badly hurt."

There was no answer. Marla was disappointed but not surprised because this was her third such attempt and given the late hour and the weather there was likely no humans out near this burial ground which was once used by the ancient Martian race. She stopped. Being a medical doctor, Marla starred back down at the body of her husband but even with her medical skill she was unable to determine what was wrong with him

"My dear and handsome Dominic!" she cried. "If only you listened to me earlier when I tried to warn you about that terrible stone or if I didn't act to rashly when you did not believe me then you would be well and we would not be in this situation."

Her gloved hand came to his face. With one of the dainty fingers, Marla rubbed his cheeks and could sense through the fabric that Dominic's skin was as cold as ice which made no sense to her but figuring out how to help him needed to take priority and so she forced those details out of her mind.

"Oh Eli," she said. "I wish I knew what was wrong with you and I wish I knew how to help you but I don't."

Marla gulped. She realized there was a way to do so but that would require her to abandon him and leave him behind in this most terrifying place, which she did not want to do. More tears formed. As Marla debated within herself how best to help the man, to whom she was married, she found herself replaying within her mind the events, which lead to this predicament.

The sand came down hard. Thankfully the intensity of the storm which attacked the makeshift city which consisted of the settlements made from the converted hulls of the early colony ships and the ancient towns and dwellings of the no longer native Martians was mitigated by the efforts of the previous generations to terraform the planet to resemble humanity's ancestral world. That did little to help Dominic or Marla. They made their way through the burial field because they were taking a short cut through it on their way back to their housing. complex Marla's heart raced. As they moved through the long rows of graves and burial plots, she was terrified not only of being in this place but by the strange illumination which she sensed was not coming from above them even though Mar's two moon of Demos and Phobos were in alignment with the planet but within this area. Her high heels dragged beneath her. Together all of this caused Marla to be worried that something terrible would happen in here but she was not certain if would be to just one of them or instead to both of them.

"Eli!" she shouted. "We've got to get out of here."

"We're almost there," Dominic retorted. "We've got to keep going."

"Eli, we've got to go back."

"It will not be much further because

"We've got to get out of this weather."

"It'll not be long now, then we'll be safe and warm again."

"Taking one of the air shuttle buses would be quick and safer."

"Our building is just on the other side, now come on."

"Yes, dear."

Marla gulped. She wanted to argue against his plan in a more assertive manner but instead she merely went along because she could not devise a means of explaining her fear to him. The couple continued their trek. Despite her terror she was taken aback by how similar the surrounding burial spaces were in design and construction to those on Earth and she was briefly amazed at how these were still intact although they were all several millions of years to several billions of years old. She thought. Centuries ago, the initial terraforming efforts did more than create a breathable atmosphere or take dried up sea and river beds and turn them into ones which were filled with green and blue rivers but also exposed abandoned cities and outposts which predated the first human settlements on the surface of Mars and with them were found monuments and the resting places of the dead all of which indicated that Mars once possessed the ability to life support life but also housed it. That race was now extinct. No human colonists or human scientists knew the cause or the reason for this or the precise date at which the former owners of the world perished but just that it occurred several millions of years ago which meant the end of it would have occurred sometime when humans were still dwelling in caves.

For the last few weeks an endless collection of storms raged. Tonight was the first beautiful night and since each half of the marriage understood they were starting to suffer from cabin fever and so they decided to out to dinner and on the way back the freak downpour of sand began and so it was Dominic's choice to take a short cut for their dwelling was on the other side of this cemetery. Marla wished she did not choose to don a dress and heels for this event. Her face was hit by the wind. After her mind clear she gazed ahead. In doing so her optics lay upon a large coffin. From this distance, she could not infer much about it but she knew at once that there was something truly evil about it because it was filled with an unusual and bright shade of gold, which pierced the sand front. Yes sand. Now in winter in addition to snowing sand also at times rained down on the planet.

"Marla," Dominic called. "Where are you?"

"I'm right behind you but I can barely see you."

"It's the same with me."

"It must be the sand."

"I want you to stay close because I don't want to lose you."

"Yes, dear."

The couple forged ahead. One of Marla's eyes continued to observe the imposing structure and as they came closer to it, she could study it in more detail. It was long. The sides of it were decorated in engravings and it was rectangular and behind it was a large marker, which was in the shape of a tall letter T, and arranged around it was a set of small stones which generated a strange bright light. They would pass it soon. Marla's eyes blinked. Her hands clenched at both sides of her body and her chest felt as if it were tightening, because she realized her first assumption was wrong for, she now knew it lay along their course and that they would soon be standing upon this structure's base. Within her chest her heart pounded. There was no doubt to Marla that she feared this tomb most of all because it confirmed the horrific notions running through her head that some dark fate would befall her or Dominic if they encountered it.

Marla stopped.

Her eyes fixated on the burial box.

They must avoid it. At all costs.

"Eli!" she shouted. "We've got to get out of here now."

"I agreed."

"We've got to get away from that tomb."

"Which one?"

Marla found she could not speak. Instead, she merely bent her arm and used one finger to point ahead towards the dreadful entity.

"Don't worry," Dominic countered, "that possess no threat to us."

"You doubt me?"

"When it comes to that I do because it's simply an old tomb."

"You're wrong."

"I think your fears are clouding your judgment."

"I'll prove it to you, just stay here."

With that, Marla walked forward. Dominic watched but knew it was his duty as her husband to protect her from any danger which might befall her and to prevent her from committing a grave act which might cost her life because no one yet fully understand the Martian burial rites or what might happen to someone who violated the sanctity of whoever was buried under that funeral pillar. A few seconds elapsed. He chased after her but was unable to reach her until she was almost upon the coffin and when he stretched out his arm towards her but as Marla was still annoyed at him for her lack of faith in her she pulled away. That was a fatal mistake. It resulted in the tips of her high heels touching the base of the tomb and as both of his feet were placed upon tomb's base Marla's greatest fear began to unfold because all of the area began to shimmer before it started to glow. Dominic quickly reacted. He pushed Marla out of the way and she spun upon the points and arches of her shoes but before he could do more than take a step backwards, there was a bright flash which startled him. The affect upon his love was greater. While she desired to come to his aid, she found she could not because she was paralyzed by her fear which locked into place on the red and orange sand.

All she could do was watch.

Dominic was hit by the full blast.

He stumbled briefly. In the process, he turned. He fell down towards the ground and landed on his chest.

That ended Marla's trance. She found her feet moving in her high heel boots and felt the sides of her dress rubbing against her legs as her petite Asian body, she was less than five feet in height, as she passed over the ground. Soon she was at her man's side. "Dominic!" she shouted. "Dominic, speak to me. Please say something to, say anything at all."

He made no response. Marla got down on both knees and starred down at to examine him using the medical training she learned in medical and learn that his skin was pale but despite that for some reason he did not react to her presence or speak to her or even budge an inch, which confused her.

Something hit Marla's face. As it brought her back to the present, which she understood was the wind and it was accompanied by more flakes of snow. A decision was made. Because none were responding to her summons for aid, she must temporally leave her man and go off in search of medical assistance for him.

"I'm sorry, Eli," she confessed. "I'm sorry but as much as I don't want to do this, I've got no choice."

Her lips planted a kiss on Dominic's very cold cheek. She shuddered. Afterwards, Marla released her hold on his physical being, and she bore witness as Dominic fell down a few inches onto the ground where he remained. Within Marla, the flow of blood through her veins suddenly stopped and as she stood there her skin abruptly lost all of the color in it. She knew why. As the man she loved gazed into her soul with his dark eyes, Marla felt that it was not warm or lovely as it was before because it to her to be unnatural.

"I'm sorry," Hanna muttered. "I'll be back as soon as I can."

She blew him a kiss. Of course, Dominic could not return the gesture. Still, it made her feel better about what she must do and so after composing herself, Marla turned and ran out of the burial field hoping that against all odds she could find someone, who could render whatever aid her man required.

"Help!" Marla shouted. "Help, my husband, he's been hurt and he needs help."

Soon she faded into the night.

Back in the graveyard, trickles of sand went down Dominic's form. It would matter not if Marla was successful or not because unknown to either half of the couple the grave, which they encountered belonged to an ancient witch. Long before humans learned how to travel through space, she committed horrible acts on her home world which led to her being tried by the members of her coven but before the punishment could be dealt to her, she fled to Earth where she performed horrible acts before she was retrieved and brought back to Mars to be executed. That was done through her being burned at the stake. However, if Marla remained in the grave yard, she would have witnessed a strange vent occur because Dominic's body was covered in light and now a translucent outline resembling his body appeared before it for this was his soul.

"I look peaceful," Dominic noted, "But I also look as if I'm dead."

"That's because you are," a voice said. In response Dominic turned and he starred at a faceless creature which possessed a vaguely defined form but while it was clearly a male it was also not human and when Dominic noticed the wings sticking out from the back this entity was identified as belonging to one of the orders which composed the heavenly hosts which served the being who created him and his beloved.

"What are you doing here?" Dominic asked.

"I have been with your kind since you first roamed your native planet."

"How can you be on Mars?"

"My kind and I travel wherever the sons of Adam and the daughters of Eve travel or settle or dwell."

"Who are you?'

"My name is known to you, from your holy text."

"You have the advantage over me."

"Look closer at me son of Man."

Dominic did so. If he were still living his heart would ceased to work and blood would have spread through his veins because the arms and the face fluctuated in their shape along with the color of skin and its texture. That caused him to search his memory. In one second the answer was found and to his horror given everything which he observed and which experience he was forced to conclude this could only be one such angel because it was the angel of death.

"Why are you here?"

"To perform my duty."

"Which is?"

"To escort you to the next stage of your existence."

"I'm confused, I don't understand how I came to here."

"Very well then."

A groan ran through the angel's form. He explained how the magical powers contained in this region was encased within a set of magical charms to prevent any vandals or any allies of the fallen witch from retrieving or removing her body parts and it did not matter that Dominic was not a magical being or user because once Marla stepped upon the base the defenses were activated and due to his actions, his soul was removed from his body.

"Can I return to my body?" Dominic questioned.

"No."

"Surely you have the ability to do so."

"That is beyond my powers."

"What do you mean?"

"I am embodied only with those necessary for the task which I have been required to perform since the dawn of time."

"What about my wife?"

"She shall learn you are dead in due course."

"Can I return to visit her?"

"Perhaps at times given the right situation."

"Will she be able to see me?"

"No but she will sense your presence."

"Will I ever be able to be with her again."

"Not until she herself has passed on from this plane of existence, now come it's time to take the new home in which you shall reside for all of eternity."

The two vanished.


Sometime later Marla returned to the cemetery and her running came to a stop at Dominic's body. "He's here!" she shouted. "He's right where I left him."

She bent down and examined him but found no change

in his condition but when she started to think a friendly hand placed itself upon her shoulder and prompted her to step aside allowing the friendly medic she encountered earlier and who returned with her to bend over the stiff body. This person's name was Joseph Galen. He was part of an archeology team which was conducting research into the ancient Martian medical techniques but while he worked Marla stood there and watched. "Well?" she questioned. "Can you do anything for him?"

"It's doubtful," Joseph answered.

"What do you mean?"

"I'm not finding any pulse or any sign that he's breathing."

"That can't be."

"I think he's dead."

"No."

"There is no sign of life left in the body, but I'll need to use the equipment back at basecamp to confirm it."

Joseph picked up Dominic's body. "Come on," he called, "we shouldn't stay out here much longer."

"He can't, he can't..." Marla stuttered, "he can't be dead."

"There's nothing that be done here at least back at the camp we can keep his body comfortable until a proper burial can be arranged for it."

# An Interview with Daniel DiQuinzio

WHEN DID YOU START WRITING AND WHY?

I thought I had something to say and I hope I could eventually earn money on the side from doing so.

WHICH AUTHORS OR BOOKS OR MEDIA INFLUENCED YOU THE MOST AS A WRITER?

Orson Scott Card, Larry Niven, Robert E. Howard, H.P. Lovecraft, Ray Bradbury.

WHICH AUTHORS OR BOOKS OR MEDIA HAD THE BIGGEST IMPACT ON YOU AS A PERSON?

C.S. Lewis, Bob Budiansky who was the initial writer for the original marvel *Transformers* comics along with Simon Furman who wrote the original marvel U.K. *Transformer* comics and was very likely the best *Transformers* comics writers, as well as classic *Star Trek*, Larry Niven and Robert E. Heinlein and in terms of my political beliefs Milton Friedman, Friedrich Hayek, Ludwig Von Mises, and William F. Buckley.

WHICH OF YOUR ORIGINAL TWELVE PROMPT STORIES ARE YOU MOST PLEASED WITH?

*Snowy Morning Closings* and *Green Timbers* as these were two of the first stories which I ever wrote and spent years trying to sell them.

WHICH OF YOUR ORIGINAL TWELVE PROMPT STORIES DID YOU FIND THE MOST DIFFICULT TO WRITE?

*Corpse on the Tombstone* as I was going through a difficult period in my life and this story cut very close to home for me.

WHAT BOOK ON WRITING DO YOU RECOMMEND?

*Plotto* by William Wallace Cook and *Writing Fantasy & Science Fiction: How to Create Out-of-This-World Novels and Short Stories* by Orson Scott Card.

WHAT ADVICE WOULD YOU GIVE TO AN UNPUBLISHED WRITER?

You must write the type of the stories that you love and you must seek opportunity where others have neglected responsibility.

DO YOU HAVE A "DREAM PROJECT" AS A WRITER? WHAT WOULD IT BE?

Either writing a film adaptation of Fred Saberhagen's *Berserker* series or writing an animated tv show which is a sequel to the original *Transformers* cartoon which is either set between the end of the second season and *Transformers: The Movie* or between the miniseries *The Rebirth* which was the fourth season and the sequel series *Beast Wars: Transformers.*

YOUR STORIES WILL BE PUBLISHED IN A SET OF PROMPT COLLECTIONS WITH THE OTHER THIRD GENERATION AUTHORS BUT ALSO AS A COLLECTION OF JUST YOUR OWN WORK. DID YOU HAVE A CONSCIOUS THEME FOR YOUR PERSONAL COLLECTION?
I did not.

WHO DO YOU WRITE FOR AND HOW DOES IT DRIVE YOU TO CREATE?
I write the type of stories that I loved reading when I was younger or that I loved watching on tv as a child.

OPTIMALLY, WE'RE ALWAYS GROWING AND IMPROVING AS AUTHORS. TALK ABOUT HOW YOU GREW OR CHANGED AS A WRITER OVER THE COURSE OF CREATING YOUR STORIES FOR *PROMPT: THE THIRD GENERATION.*
Learning how to vary writing style as well as the manner in which I open my stories and varying the length of paragraphs.

IMAGINE THE PERFECT COVER FOR YOUR PERSONAL COLLECTION. DESCRIBE IT... EVEN IF IT'S IMPOSSIBLE.
A dark mysterious planet floating in space with a large translucent Spector hovering over it.

9 798889 439048 2